MW01026874

A SEVEN WORLD NOVEL

USA TODAY BESTSELLING AUTHOR

DANNIKA DARK

All Rights Reserved
Copyright © 2015 Dannika Dark

First Print Edition
ISBN-13: 978-1517165895
ISBN-10: 151716589X

Formatting: Streetlight Graphics

No part of this book may be reproduced, distributed, or transmitted in any form
or by any means, or stored in a database retrieval system, without the prior
written permission of the author. You must not circulate this book in any format.
Thank you for respecting the rights of the author.

This is a work of fiction. Any resemblance of characters to actual persons, living
or dead, is purely coincidental.

Professionally edited by Victory Editing and Red Adept.
Cover design by Dannika Dark. All stock purchased.

www.dannikadark.net
Fan page located on Facebook

Also By Dannika Dark:

THE MAGERI SERIES
Sterling
Twist
Impulse
Gravity
Shine

NOVELLAS
Closer

THE SEVEN SERIES
Seven Years
Six Months
Five Weeks
Four Days
Three Hours
Two Minutes

SEVEN WORLD
Charming

Dear Reader,

Charming was originally planned to be a novella in the Seven series; however, it took on a life of its own and unfolded into a full-length novel. *Charming* can be read as a stand-alone. In the Seven series timeline, it falls between *Two Minutes* and *One Second*. There are no major spoilers in this book, should you decide to read the Seven series at a later time.

Happy reading.

PROLOGUE

I T HAD BEEN A WEEK since Prince visited the Weston pack and offered a ride home to their enchanting guest, Nadia Kozlov. Since then, he hadn't been able to stop thinking about her, and not just because of her golden locks and regal demeanor. During introductions, he'd been startled to discover that Nadia was the daughter of an old friend he hadn't set eyes on in over two hundred years—a ghost from his past who still haunted him in quiet moments.

His life had been a long one, even in the Shifter world. Prince was not only one of the most influential alpha Packmasters in Austin, Texas, but also of royal blood. Pureblood, to be exact. That meant his lifespan was much longer than the average wolf, and he had many more lifetimes to live. Prince played with the gold chain on a green banker's lamp, lost in the memories of another life.

Centuries ago, Prince had left Italy and returned to his homeland of Russia, not realizing the Shifters in the region were on the brink of war. Those were different times when powerful immortals kept Shifters as slaves. Russia was a free zone where all Breeds were equal, but as more and more Shifters settled and claimed land, resentment grew.

He'd forged a friendship with a powerful Packmaster named Alexei Kozlov, whom Prince called Alex. Both alphas were descended from royalty—powerful Shifters with the purest bloodline. But they soon realized they had much more than heritage in common and spent many nights by a warm fire, toasting to longevity and discussing the political changes underfoot. Like Prince, Alex was also a single alpha with no children.

Prince recalled a conversation they'd had.

"It's only a matter of time before we lose our stronghold," Alex had said one evening, poking at the dying embers of the fire, which had been burning for hours. "We can either flee or organize a resistance, but we must make a decision. The peace treaty won't hold for long in our territory."

Prince had turned his attention toward the window, watching his reflection in the glass. "I caught two of my men in treasonous acts, selling information to a powerful Mage. I don't know who I can trust anymore."

Alex nodded, stroking his long mustache. "That is why we choose to fight those who would oppress us, or else our packmates will be easily swayed by a few rubles."

"My pack is strong, but we are few. We cannot take on a large pack, let alone an army of Vampires."

Alex had turned to face him, firelight casting his dark shadow on the floor. "It's not the Vampires you have to worry about, my friend. It's the Mage who wants your head on his mantel."

After their discussion, Prince had briefly considered returning to Italy, but there wasn't much land left for Shifters, and he couldn't be certain they still had their freedom. The world had always been mad, but it was as if they were losing the last sanctuaries where a Shifter could live free. While some animals such as bears could go undetected and live as rogues, Prince was a wolf, and packs attracted attention.

Barbarism was seeping into the minds of intellectuals—ancients who recognized an opportunity to acquire wealth by stealing it. When the war began, the Shifters fought valiantly against their Mage adversaries, but most were outnumbered. Shifters who weren't killed were driven out.

Vladimir Romanov, a Mage who served under a powerful general, had organized a brutal attack against Prince's men. Vlad had always been envious of Prince's growing power in the region and had threatened him numerous times. Prince vividly remembered the cold press of mud against his knees as he was forced to watch while his pack was chained and carted off to be sold. Alphas were usually executed, so Prince wasn't loaded onto the cart with his packmates. Packmasters were considered a baneful influence, and aside from that, an alpha would never submit to slavery. However, Vlad's intentions for him were far more sinister.

Amid the chaos following Prince's capture, a large horse appeared, wet snow tangled in his black mane. Alex slid off the saddle, mud splashing beneath his feet. Guards rushed him when he held up his hands in surrender.

"I was not surprised to hear the news," he growled at Vlad. "Who is next on your list? *My* pack?"

Vlad pulled his ushanka tighter so the dark fur covered his red ears. "Did you honestly think the treaty we signed would last? That was just to keep you from rebelling until we were ready to put the animals in their cages."

Alex had always been held in high regard in that region because he'd built solid relationships with other Breeds. In a move Prince would never have seen coming, Alex offered his own freedom in exchange for Prince's release. Not only that, but he relinquished his entire fortune on the condition Vlad would not enslave his own pack, but show mercy and allow them to flee the country.

Prince stood up to object and was struck in the head with a blunt object. When he awoke, he was lying in the back of a horse-drawn cart, well outside territory lines. Banished while his pack met a horrific fate, Prince was given a warning by the driver, who stated that if Vlad so much as heard about him crossing the border, he would take Alex's head. Prince was profoundly affected by his friend's selfless act, forever remaining in his debt.

Prince had scattered his wealth in many places—something he'd kept secret from even Alex. Prince's father had taught him valuable lessons, and one of them was that you can trust a man with your life more than you can your money. It was time to collect his fortune and start over.

He'd been reluctant to leave Europe for the new world since Europe had always been home, but war had taken its toll, and the outlook was bleak. Winter was bitterly cold in Russia, and the warmer climates of distant continents and the hope of peace called to him. Once he'd made the decision to journey to America, it had taken him months to gather his fortune from hidden locations. Currency often changed in value, but gold never went out of style. America had more land, and while Shifters were still held in slavery in many populated territories, there were rumors of undiscovered land that stretched beyond the imagination where Shifters lived free. Starting over wasn't easy, but he'd worked hard to acclimate to a new culture, build alliances, and lose his accent.

Prince shifted in his chair, looking around his lavish surroundings and thinking back to those tumultuous times. He never heard from Alex again and had assumed him dead… until a few days ago when he'd run into Nadia Kozlov.

A knock sounded at the door—one he was expecting.

CHAPTER 1

"**S**IRE, YOUR VISITOR'S IN THE sitting room," Stover informed him in a thick Scottish accent. Russell was Prince's second-in-command—and on the receiving end of countless jokes because of his name. Every Christmas, the men honored him with a box of assorted Russell Stover chocolates. Russell would conjure a smile and graciously accept the gift, although Prince could tell the novelty had worn off decades ago. But a man who complains only puts a bigger target on his back, so he wisely left it alone. Besides, a man could hardly object to a few taunts when it earned him confectioneries in return.

Prince rose from his chair and crossed the room, the soles of his shoes tapping heavily against the marble floor. He'd been waiting upstairs in a quiet study all afternoon, unable to read or put his thoughts to rest after sending one of his men for Nadia. Their brief encounter had ended abruptly when she'd received a business call that continued for the rest of the car ride. So to remedy their abbreviated meeting, Prince had invited her over for drinks, hoping to finally get answers about what had become of his friend Alex.

"This is *quite* a mansion," Nadia remarked from the first floor below, speaking with a lovely Russian accent. Every sound was amplified because of the large space.

Prince descended the stairs with a casual swagger, averting his wayward gaze from her beautiful legs. Her white business skirt suited her in a way that left a man thinking about anything but business.

"I'm pleased you could come on such short notice, Miss Kozlov."

When she bowed, her silky blond hair slipped forward. It was past her shoulders and as straight as could be. "I cannot help but notice how you enjoy saying my name."

"This way." Prince took her arm and led her toward the parlor at the other end of the rotunda.

Her eyes soaked in the magnificence of his mansion—the marble floors, exquisite paintings, golden light that showered down from the skylight above, and silence. Not all Packmasters could claim to have a quiet house, but it was a luxury Prince appreciated. When not performing their jobs, his pack preferred to either congregate in one of the social rooms or let their wolves roam the property. The only ones allowed to make noise within the main rooms were the children, but even they were quiet and respectful when he passed through the room.

As soon as they entered the parlor, Nadia whirled around dramatically and put her hands on her hips. "Do you really know my father, or was this a ploy to get me alone?"

Prince closed the door. "Does he still live?"

She shrugged indifferently. "Last I heard."

"When is the last time you spoke?"

Her finely shaped brows arched as she turned on her heel and poured herself a glass of white wine at the long table against the wall.

Prince watched with mild curiosity as she crossed the gold marble floor and stepped onto the oversized white rug in the center of the room. He often used this room to impress his guests by flaunting his wealth. She glanced up at the crystal chandelier that hung from the high ceiling. It wasn't the only source of light, as track lighting ran along the outer edges. Nadia chose to sit in one of the chairs instead of the gold couch, which he had hoped she would do. He preferred sitting beside female companions when conversing.

Nadia sipped her wine, leaving a red lipstick stain on the rim of the glass. She set it down on a table and then looked about the room. "I must say that pack life treats you well. It always benefits the Packmaster more than his packmates."

He strode across the area rug and sat on the edge of the sofa, Nadia to his right. "And where do you think my pack lives? They enjoy the same accommodations I do. The same food, the same land, the same roof above."

"But not to the degree you do."

He laced his fingers together. "Is that what keeps you from joining a pack, Miss Kozlov?"

She looked at him unabashedly, her pale brown eyes sparkling beneath the light. "Precisely. I have no desire to share what is mine."

He pursed his lips, admiring a woman who spoke the truth. It was a quality he'd always been attracted to, even over looks or the purity of a woman's blood. "Perhaps you do not aspire to a high enough position."

"Is that an invitation?" Her red lips turned up in a smile. "I'm a gregarious woman who enjoys going out at night. Most alphas wouldn't find me an ideal mate because I prefer having a good time over staying home and bonding with a pack. I'm afraid my social habits wouldn't change if I chose to mate."

"Why would you desire the company of strangers when there are plenty of Shifters within a pack to keep you company?"

This time she really did laugh, though she did it with closed lips so that it was more of a snicker. "What makes you think I'd find those of my caliber within the house? I don't seek the company of just *anyone*. I enjoy intellectual conversation, dancing, dining, and spending time in the VIP lounges of all the trendy clubs."

"In search of what?"

She crossed her legs, and when they brushed together, her skin made a soft hiss, sending a shiver up his spine. Her legs were undeniably long and feminine with just the right amount of curve at the hip. He couldn't tell if her eyelashes were false, but they were thick and black. They fanned over brown eyes that shifted with the light—sometimes taking on a stormy color. Nadia was lovely—exquisite features, like a fairy. It was hard to believe someone like Alex could have produced such a creature.

"You make plenty of assumptions," she replied, turning the gold watch on her wrist and giving it a cursory glance. "So tell me, why did you invite me here? Are you assessing me for personal reasons, or did you want information on my father?"

He widened his legs and leaned back, taking a moment to ponder her question. Nadia wanted him to choose, and he had to tread carefully since both topics were of equal priority.

"I consider myself fortunate to share the company of a beautiful woman who is also the daughter of an old friend."

"Well played." She set her glass down after another sip and angled her body in his direction. "I've never had a close relationship with my father."

Intrigued, Prince leaned forward. "By choice or circumstance?"

Nadia twirled an emerald ring on her finger. "My father had priorities and was always a busy man. I'm not yet fifty, if that gives you a timeline." Shifters aged slowly, and Nadia looked like a delicate flower in her midtwenties. "Life was different then, as you must know. So much has changed for Shifters in just the past twenty years. But back then, his focus was on his pack."

A smile touched his lips. "So he's rebuilt?"

Her brows drew together. "Rebuilt what? My father was a rogue until my mother came along. Then he decided to settle down and become a Packmaster."

It seemed Alex had kept secrets from his daughter. "And your mother?"

She sighed dramatically, and her gaze drifted up to the opulent crystal chandelier. "My mother…" Nadia's eyes glittered for a moment. "My mother was underwhelmed by the monotony of pack life and left her family to mate a powerful alpha."

Prince's lip curled in when she didn't use the term *Packmaster*. "A rogue? She chose a *rogue* over your father?"

Nadia glanced at her watch again. "Yes. As I said, she had different priorities and a change of heart. I can't blame the woman for wanting more from life. My father did an adequate job raising me, and now look where I am. I'm an artifacts dealer who specializes in rarities. No one knows as much as I do about the value of old pieces, and no one has my connections to match buyers with sellers. It's not as if we have an auction house among the Breed. My father raised an independent woman, so I have little concern over men who flash their judgmental eyes at me. The only thing I lack is a good man." She sighed thoughtfully and lifted her glass of wine. "I had hoped things would work out between Denver and me. He and I are similar in that we both—"

"*Denver?*" Prince blurted out. He belonged to the Weston pack and worked as a bartender, hardly worthy of a woman such as Nadia. "You would have mated with a low-ranking wolf?"

She licked a drop of wine from her lip and set the glass down again. "Do I look like a woman who is searching for a man to offer me the comforts of money?"

What exactly was she searching for? *An obedient man? A plaything?* Prince bristled at the idea because Nadia was descended from nobility—one of the purest Shifter bloodlines in Europe. He and Alex came from two of the oldest generations of powerful Shifters—their life spans would stretch twice as long as other wolves. Because of that rare purity, importance had always been placed on not diluting their family line by mating with an inferior Shifter. There were few purebloods, and they were still royalty even if others were oblivious. So finding out about Nadia's existence had sent a sliver of hope that he might have found his perfect mate.

Finally.

"Have you taken up residency in your mind, or would you like to join the living?" she asked. "I have a meeting with a client in an hour."

Prince rose to his feet, disheartened.

Nadia caught his look. "I'll tell you what—why don't you come to my place for dinner tonight? I don't work in the evening, and that will give you plenty of time to tell me about how you know my father. We'll have *hours*," she said, uncrossing her legs. "Although I hope you don't want to spend *all* that time talking about him."

He gently took her hand, noticing how delicate her fingers were. Her fingernails were a deep shade of violet, and he kissed the knuckles on her right hand, all while keeping his eyes on hers. She rose to her feet, and the sweet scent of her perfume swirled between them.

"I adore a gentleman. No later than seven, and bring a bottle of wine."

He arched a brow. "That I can do. Would you prefer red or white?"

"Surprise me."

CHAPTER 2

RINCE KNOCKED ON THE APARTMENT door for the second time, a bottle of wine in one hand and impatience in the other. A short, round woman with a fluffy white dog passed by him. She wobbled back and forth from what looked like a bad hip, pausing briefly to praise Mr. Teasley for sniffing Prince's Italian leather shoes and showing what a good dog he was. After she went into her apartment, Prince bent down to wipe the stray dog hairs off his pant leg.

When the door swung open, he found himself at eye level with the most remarkable knees.

"That's an interesting way to greet a woman," Nadia said with a sultry chuckle. "I'd apologize for having you stand out in the hall so long, but I prefer to keep my men waiting. Come inside."

She turned away and Prince stood erect, straightening his suit jacket and closing the door behind him.

"These are modest accommodations, Miss Kozlov. I thought you had money."

Nadia was clipping on a pair of gold earrings while standing at the entranceway to her living room. "An intelligent woman doesn't spend it all in one place. And never assume, Mister…"

"Prince."

"You want me to call you Mr. Prince?"

"It's the only name I have. Call me what you wish."

Nadia put on her other earring, fastening the back. "As I was saying, Prince, I've purchased all the apartments on this floor as an investment. Well, except for the woman's down the hall. I can't seem to get her to sell, but since she doesn't bother me, I can patiently wait her out. I have all the privacy I need with the convenience of living in the city near my clients. I've even renovated one of the apartments to allow my wolf to run." Once she got herself together, she examined him closely. "You are a handsome man. Your features are very distinguished—something I don't see very often unless I'm in Europe."

If Prince were a man of humility, he might have blushed. But it was a compliment he'd received often from women. He was a Shifter in his prime—seven hundred years old, but he appeared to be in his late thirties. He still had many more years ahead of him, and hoped he would age as well as his father had. His long hair didn't appeal to many women, so he pulled it back in a tight band for a distinguished look. It drew attention to his unique eye coloring. Prince was born with one brown and one sapphire-colored eye, and while most would have concealed such a defect with contacts or hidden it behind long hair, he had chosen not to. A man who hid his differences was a man who considered himself inferior.

"There is only one object in this room worth admiring," he replied smoothly.

Her gaze dragged down to his hand and she smiled. "The expensive wine?"

They both jumped when a fist pounded against the door. Nadia glanced at her watch, and when a look of confusion crossed her face, Prince turned the wine bottle in his hand and held it like a weapon.

The pounding continued and a woman sang, "I know you're in there!"

Nadia's eyes not only rolled to the back of her head, but her eyelids fluttered. "Of *all* times… This is not the place… Always doing this," she murmured under her breath while she unlocked the door.

In a swift motion, Nadia swung the door open. A woman with leather pants, attitude, and black tresses in unkempt waves filled the doorway. She leaned on the doorjamb. "'Bout time you opened the door. I was starting to fossilize. Something smells good."

Nadia extended her arm in front of the woman, blocking her entrance. "*Impeccable* timing, as always."

"I see you still haven't dropped your accent," she muttered, ducking below Nadia's arm and sauntering inside. Before Prince realized it, the woman plucked the bottle from his hand and turned it around to read the label. "Yummy."

"Katarina, I have a guest. Is there somewhere you can go until—"

"Nope." Katarina held the bottle to her mouth, biting the end in what looked like an attempt to open it.

Prince grew agitated. The thought of this woman breaking her teeth on a nine-hundred-dollar bottle of wine made him wince. He took it away from her. "It's sealed with a cork."

"Ah," she said with a snap of her fingers. "I should have known. Nadia likes the fancy stuff that doesn't come with a screw top. Don't you, Nads?"

"Don't call me that," Nadia bit out, slamming the door. "What sewer did you crawl out of today?"

"Hey, is that any way to greet your long-lost—"

Nadia cleared her throat. "Shall I just get my wallet?"

The woman raked her fingers through her hair and turned around. "Now I'm insulted. I only borrowed money *once*, and I paid it back the next day."

When she faced Prince, he took a step back. Confusion swam in his eyes as he gripped the arch dividing the living room and front entrance.

"What's the matter, never seen a carbon copy before?"

His eyes darted between Nadia and Katarina—the resemblance was uncanny. They were identical twins. Same warm eyes, same flawless skin and heart-shaped face, same attractive figure. The main difference was that Katarina had dyed her hair black, and it looked like the only thing that brushed it was the wind. When Nadia approached her sister, they registered at the same height, and yet the differences in personality between the two were striking. Katarina wore leather pants and a black shirt that revealed an inch of midriff. Her black boots were scuffed, and she didn't paint her nails or wear makeup that he could see. Not that she needed any; her skin was luminous.

Prince had always been fascinated by the way a person's body language spoke before they did. Each woman had a confident stance, but in different ways. Katarina's pose was smug and nonchalant, whereas Nadia seemed ever-aware of her ladylike posture.

"Take a picture, it'll last longer," Katarina said with a snort. She slung her right arm around Nadia's shoulder, waiting for Prince to respond.

Nadia stiffly gazed at Prince with an apologetic look in her eyes.

Prince bowed slightly. "Pleased to make your acquaintance, Katarina Kozlov."

"Kat."

He flicked his glance up.

She jutted her hip to the side and smiled softly. "Everyone calls me Kat. Well, everyone except my own flesh and blood, but she's excused."

"I apologize," Nadia said to Prince. "We can do this another time."

Prince slid her a reassuring smile. "If you didn't prepare enough for three, we can always share a bottle of wine."

"Sounds perfect!" Kat exclaimed.

A flutter of amusement rolled through Prince, but he concealed his smile. She didn't have an accent like Nadia, and her personality was a force to be reckoned with.

Nadia frowned and looked toward the kitchen. "I only baked two quails."

Kat wrinkled her nose. "Quail? No, thanks. Why don't you two gobble that up and I'll just order a pizza."

"And *who* will pay?" Nadia asked.

Prince quickly spoke up. "I'll cover the expense."

"Swell!" Kat said jauntily, walking past him. "I left my credit cards behind, and I'm low on cash." She suddenly whirled around and held up her index finger. "I want the largest pizza they sell that has three kinds of meat. Extra everything. Oh, and a two-liter bottle of soda with a side order of garlic breadsticks." She nibbled on the tip of her thumb. "And if they have anything sweet, I'll take it. Cinnamon sticks, brownies, whatever."

"What if I just order it all?" Prince suggested.

In a motion too fast to track, Kat pounced forward and wrapped her arms around his neck, gazing up at him with provocative eyes. "Then I just might mate with you." Her eyes flicked back and forth between his. "Say, you have different color eyes."

"Katarina!" Nadia gasped. "That's enough. Why don't you clean yourself up while I put dinner on the table?"

Kat left the room with a sullen expression, hands clasped behind her back.

"Let me apologize for my sister. She's crass and doesn't have a sense of when she's acting inappropriately."

He lightly shrugged. "I find nothing rude about stating the obvious, unless the intention is to cause emotional pain."

Strangely, Prince liked that Kat had addressed his eye color right away. Most people never mentioned it, although they would steal glimpses when they thought he wasn't looking. She didn't say it in a way that had offended him either. In fact, he'd stirred a little when she gazed into his eyes, their bodies pressed together and her arms around his neck. He'd centered his attention on her soft lips, or at least he imagined they were soft. Her breasts were *unquestionably* soft by the way they had molded against his chest, and she wasn't wearing a bra. That kind of detail rarely escaped a man's attention.

Nadia touched his arm, quieting her voice. "Katarina is like a virus. She infects people with her unsolicited opinions. I'm sure I won't have to worry about that with a man like you. You'll have to ignore half of what she says; she was raised differently than I was. She's lived in America longer and has no ambition. The only time she shows up is when she needs a place to stay for a few days."

"What does she do that she wanders around like a nomad?"

Nadia cupped her elbows. "She's a bounty hunter."

Prince's jaw slackened. "I've never met a female bounty hunter."

"Now you have. She won't settle down with a job that doesn't involve slamming someone's head against the hood of a car. It pays well, but she's not as wealthy as she could be because Katarina gives away too much of it to Breed orphanages and God knows what else. Why don't you go home and we'll do this again another time?"

Because then Prince wouldn't get to learn about the peculiar offspring that Alex had produced. "Would you like me to assist you in the kitchen?"

She laughed with her lips pressed tightly together and began to pull off his suit jacket. "Take a seat in the living room and make yourself comfortable. It shouldn't be long."

"Yummy." Kat folded a giant wedge of pizza in half and took a hungry bite, causing an avalanche of melted cheese and meat to slide off. She used her fingers to pinch the cheese in half, winding it up and placing it back on her pizza. The aroma of spices was heavy in the air, and after filling her mouth, she licked the sauce from her fingertips. She hadn't even bothered to use a plate but instead had set the pizza box in front of her and ripped off the top.

Prince shifted in his chair and examined his glazed quail.

A burst of laughter flew out of Kat's mouth when she looked at his plate. "I *love* the position you put her in, Nads. It looks like the poor bird's about to get laid."

Nadia shaded her eyes with one hand, concealing the blush that tinted her cheeks. She was sitting at the head of the table to Prince's left, with Kat directly in front of him.

"I'm not trying to be rude," Kat continued. "I just thought you were supposed to tie up the legs or something. Say, did you ever get a TV? I don't want to miss all my favorite shows."

Nadia cut through her asparagus. "It sounds like you need to buy a home of your own. Then you can have all the television sets you desire."

Kat gave her a frosty look while picking a sausage off her pizza. "I just thought it would be nice to watch TV while you're out toasting the town. I'm not much of a reader—not that you have any books," she said with a chuckle. Then she turned her attention to Prince. "I may not look like it, but I'm the homebody in this family. Nadia likes to party all night, but I guess you know that already. When I'm not working, I just like to kick off my shoes, snuggle up on the sofa with a warm blanket, and have something to take my mind off everything. *I Love Lucy* works like a charm every time."

Prince set down his fork. The way she shifted her eyes when

talking about winding down from work made him curious about how stressful it was. "What is your line of work?"

"Bounty hunter. But *shhh*. It's never a good idea to spread that kind of thing around. Most of the guys I turn in stay locked up for life, but people hold grudges for a long time. The last thing I need is someone blowing my cover, so usually the only people who find out are the ones I haul in." She chewed on the crust of her pizza and spoke with a mouthful. "It's good money, in case you're wondering. And while Nads over there thinks I do it because I enjoy beating people up, it's not about that. When I catch a criminal, I'm doing some good in the world, like taking out the trash. You know? I get to choose my cases, and I can't resist hunting down a no-good loser who touched a little kid where he shouldn't have."

A muscle twitched in Prince's cheek, and he leaned back. Just the thought of a male harming a child sent a reaction through him like fire racing up a trail of gasoline toward an explosive. "How can someone your size capture these men?"

Kat swept her dark hair back, unaware she had a dab of tomato sauce on the corner of her mouth. "I'm going to pretend I didn't hear the underlying sexism in that remark. I'm tougher than I look, and so is my wolf."

"Are you armed?"

She eyed him suspiciously and bit off another piece of her crust. "I carry a stunner because sometimes I have to track down the occasional Mage."

Stunners were weapons, usually knives, infused with magic that would paralyze a Mage if embedded in their flesh. "And what if they are not a Mage?"

"Well, as it turns out, knives come in handy with just about anyone. Except Vampires. I once paralyzed a Vamp after driving a wooden spike through his shoulder, but I don't like getting that close to them. They have a nifty trick of snapping necks with a flick of the wrist. I won't be doing *that* again," she said almost to herself, picking up a giant glob of cheese from her plate and putting it in her mouth.

Prince had never met a beautiful woman with such atrocious table manners. And yet her behavior wasn't vulgar so much as it was quirky. Kat fascinated him in a way that took him off guard. She reminded him so much of Alex.

"Are you also estranged from your father?" he asked coolly, hoping she would give him more answers than Nadia had.

The twins looked between each other and Kat dropped her pizza crust into the box. "Estranged? I've been looking for the man for the past two decades."

Prince quit chewing his food and swallowed the last bite. "Would you mind explaining?"

"While my sister wants to sit there and pretend that our father left us, I know for a fact he's in trouble. Someone took him, because he would *never* go this long without getting in touch with one of us."

Nadia rolled her eyes, and when Prince noticed, Kat followed the direction of his gaze.

"I'm sorry that you weren't daddy's girl, but that doesn't mean you have to punish him with your indifference," Kat said. "He didn't abandon us; someone *took* him. You don't have to believe me, but I'll never stop looking for him."

"And why would someone take our father? What reason could anyone have to abduct a Packmaster? Kidnapping is so Middle Ages."

"People do it every day," Kat murmured, prying another large slice of pizza from the pie.

Prince pushed his plate away, his appetite gone. "What makes you believe he's in trouble? Who would have a grudge against him that they'd risk capturing a Packmaster?"

Kat swallowed a bite from her fourth slice and sat back, patting her bloated stomach with a satisfied look on her face. "I have a couple of ideas, but nothing solid."

Nadia tapped her fingernail on her glass of white wine, the crystal ringing a high note. She looked at Prince and lowered her voice. "Remember what I said about infectious behavior?"

A hiccup from Kat drew his attention forward again.

"Seriously, are you *still* calling me a virus?" she asked Nadia. "I'm not the only rude one in this family. Having an opinion isn't a character flaw; God knows you have plenty of your own that I'm subjected to hearing. Motivating people isn't a negative trait. If I were a man, I would have been a Packmaster and you wouldn't be questioning my behavior."

Nadia held the stem of her glass. "But as it stands, you don't have any testicles that I'm aware of. Prince is a respected Packmaster with responsibilities. He's not a man you can brainwash into following your schemes."

"He's also a man of free will who happens to be sitting at this table." Kat looked at Prince, her eyes resolute. "So what do you think? Do you want to help find my father?"

Nadia threw her white cloth napkin on the table. "That's enough, Katarina. You've exceeded your wine and caloric intake."

Kat stood up and grabbed the bottle. "I don't think I've had *enough*, because I sure as hell need something to anesthetize me from the ignorance that lives within this house."

"One you're free to leave anytime."

Prince sat back and folded his arms, amused by the quarreling between two women who looked and sounded the same but were mirror opposites.

Kat took a swig of wine, settling her eyes on Nadia. "At least I make an attempt to keep a relationship with you. Maybe you don't like me swinging by unannounced, but how often do you call or come by where I'm staying? Never. I call you as often as I can, but you don't answer. Before cell phones, you used to let the answering machine screen your calls, but at least you could lie and say you weren't home. There's no excuse for you not answering my calls now, because you carry that phone wherever you go!"

Something changed in Kat's voice—a catch in her throat that snagged Prince's attention. Her anger switched to something else, and her lip trembled for a fraction of a second before she took another swig of wine and stalked out of the room. His heart clenched and he felt an unexpected compulsion to go after her. There was nothing petulant about her outburst, just an underlying sadness.

Nadia gripped his left arm. "If you'd like to go, I have no complaints."

"Not one?" he asked, placing his right hand on top of hers.

She flashed a lovely smile and tilted her head to one side. "Maybe a tiny one."

"Your life intrigues me. I never imagined Alex would have such willful, strong daughters."

"Alex?"

He nodded. "It's what I called him."

"I never did like nicknames," she said, her voice tired. "Sometimes I wish a man would take her off my hands, then maybe she wouldn't come around so often."

"You don't like your sister's company? She's your twin."

The air cooled, and Nadia retracted her hand to sip her wine. "We have nothing in common. If you don't have siblings, you wouldn't understand. The last time she came to visit, I was entertaining a group of friends. It was an upscale party until she had everyone doing shots. Then the music changed and she infected them with her riotous behavior. No one wanted her to leave."

"I've heard twins are competitive."

Nadia shook her head, resting her narrow chin on her laced fingers. "That's not it at all. Katarina is the dysfunctional one."

He smiled and glanced at the open doorway. "She seems quite functional to me."

"I think we both know what I'm talking about. There's a certain way one should aspire to live their life. Her bounty hunter title keeps her from having the negative label of being a rogue, but that's *exactly* what she is by choice."

"You don't consider yourself rogue?"

"I'm a businesswoman, settled in one place, and contribute to my community. It's hardly the same."

The soft lull of her words broke when the phone beside her plate went off. "Hello? Yes. … That's excellent. Can you send me the information in an e-mail and—" She paused, the other person's voice barely audible. "I'm eating at the moment. Can it wait?" She eyed Prince and held up one finger as she stood up and left the room.

Prince folded his cloth napkin and draped it over his half-eaten quail. Nadia was a skillful cook, but he'd been too anxious to eat, and that was an emotion Prince wasn't accustomed to. He rose from his chair and entered the dim living room. Nadia had refined taste and had put thought into how she decorated her living space. A white sofa ran along the wall to his right, and across from it, a tall curio was lit up from within.

Kat was sitting on the sofa, staring at the glass shelves. The wine bottle sat on the floor to her left. "Maybe if I pretend hard enough, the figurines will move around and entertain me," she said. "Who doesn't own a television?"

He took a seat beside her and stared at the cabinet. Light sparkled against the glass shelves inside, giving a magical aura to the figurines of women, children, and flowers. "I only have one television in my house, but it's for the pack."

Her voice softened. "You're missing out."

He slanted his eyes toward her legs. The dark leather stood out against the white couch and complemented her figure. His fingers wanted to touch the material, to know what it felt like.

"Did you bring luggage?"

"Not this time. If Nadia's in one of her moods and doesn't want to lend me a gown, I guess that means I'll be sleeping in the nude tonight."

Prince placed his hands in his lap, hoping she hadn't noticed the twitch in his pants. He silently cursed himself for behaving like a young wolf.

"So you're the boyfriend? Nadia always had good taste in men. I don't know why she won't settle down. I mean, she's got it all going on. Looks, grace, a career—but then maybe she's never been able to find a guy of her caliber. That's what people need, someone who's on the same level."

He lowered his voice to a rich timbre. "For someone who bickers with her sister, you speak highly of her."

Kat scooted down, her gaze adrift. "I love Nadia; she's all I've got in this world. We couldn't be more different, though. Sometimes I think if we weren't related by blood, she'd cut ties with me."

"I wouldn't be so sure of that."

She threw her head back and yawned. "I would."

Prince looked at her over his right shoulder, admiring the way the dim glow from the curio accented her lovely mouth and angled jaw. He considered how to best answer her previous question about his relationship with Nadia. "We just met. There's no relationship to speak of."

"Give it time. You're like peas in a pod." She leaned against his arm. "You even smell yummy. I probably smell like oil."

"You mean pizza grease?" he replied, a smile touching his lips. But when he briefly dipped his nose in her hair, he smelled something indescribably wonderful.

"No," she murmured sleepily. "My car died on the way over. I had to check the engine and got fluid all over my hands."

When Kat shivered, Prince wrapped his arm around her and she nestled against his chest. He thought about how satisfying it was to hold a woman—an affection he didn't indulge in very often, if at all.

"I'm going to have to cut our evening short," Nadia announced, strolling into the room in a pair of strappy heels. "I have a client who's in need of funds tonight, and I've got two hours to locate a buyer for his painting." She tapped her fingernail against a tooth, her gaze distant. "I'm tempted to buy it myself and sell it later so I don't have to jump through all these hoops. If you want to wait for me, I'll be back in an hour or two. It depends on how much he wants to charge. If not, then I'll understand," she said, judgment clinging to the edge of her voice.

Nadia was testing him, seeing what he was willing to do for her time and affection.

Under the circumstances, he could hardly go anywhere. Kat had somehow adhered herself to his side and was drooling on his shirt. Oddly, Nadia didn't question their cozy position.

"Perhaps I'll find a blanket for your sister and then wait on the terrace."

That pleased her. "If you get sleepy, feel free to lie down in my bed. Just make sure you've removed your clothes; I like to keep my sheets clean. I'll be back soon."

With a jingle of her keys, Nadia slipped out the front door. The second it slammed, Kat sat upright, eyes wide.

"Your sister left," he said.

She released a heavy breath.

"Tell me, why doesn't Nadia seem concerned about leaving us alone?"

Kat yawned and rubbed her eyes. "Nadia's men never want anything to do with me, and that goes both ways. She knows I'd never betray her trust. I'm a loyal wolf."

CHAPTER 3

K AT DIDN'T WANT TO IMPOSE on her sister, especially after the last visit when Nadia had kicked her out of the apartment for painting the walls pale yellow. Kat hadn't meant any harm; she'd just thought the place needed a little cheering up. What she really wanted to do was shift and relax, but she wasn't allowed to because the last time she did, her wolf had left a ton of black hairs all over Nadia's white couch.

Nadia could be a real bitch, but Kat wasn't perfect by a mile. After all, who wants to hang out with a woman who dedicates her life to tracking down thugs? When on assignment, Kat spent most of her days and nights in bars, going undercover and squeezing juicy gossip from her informants. She had to dress the part, and eventually the lines blurred on how much of it was an act and how much was really her. As long as the clothes were comfortable, she didn't care.

Granted, leather pants had their downside. As badass and sexy as they looked, they also made her legs sweat. Kat preferred distressed jeans or a pair of khakis, but unfortunately she had nothing else to wear at the moment since she'd driven into town straight from a biker bar in Shreveport.

After waking up in Prince's armpit, she'd slinked out of the room to retrieve two leftover slices of pizza from the dining table. Kat meandered into the living room and sat on the sofa beside Prince.

Prince. What kind of name was that? Tall, graceful like a panther, long hair—and Kat had always had a thing for long-haired men. On top of that, he smelled good… beneath all the cologne. Prince had a face that artists chiseled from marble, and don't get her started on his eyes. The intensity of his gaze made her talk faster than usual. Up close, the contrasting colors were arresting, and they pulled her in like magnets. Men shouldn't have eyes that sexy. Especially not with wolfish brows that sometimes slanted in a way that sent a shiver up her spine. Prince was like a knight all cleaned up and wearing a silk suit. Okay, so maybe that was a little overboard, but she definitely enjoyed the sexy image in her mind of him astride a black stallion, wielding a sword.

Nadia had picked a winner this time. Not too young, not too old, and an alpha to boot.

But Kat knew beneath all the layers of sophistication was a man like any other man. At the end of the day, he was no different than the guy selling magazines in the airport. Same basic wants and needs, even if he didn't choose to acknowledge them.

"Have a bite," she offered, handing him a slice of room-temperature pizza. "You didn't eat enough at dinner. I know this isn't exactly a four-star meal, but at least it's more edible than my sister's wild game."

He eyed the pizza skeptically. "I wouldn't go so far as to call that edible."

That was a little high and mighty. She turned to face him and waved the pizza in front of his mouth, brushing the tip against his lower lip. "Don't think I didn't notice your stomach growling earlier. What do you think lulled me to sleep? We can do this the easy way or the hard way. I prefer the hard way, but it's up to you."

Kat was joking, but much to her surprise, he took the slice from her hand and bit into it. Now *that* piqued her curiosity even more. How often do you get to see someone experience their first bite of pizza?

"Well? How is it?"

The lines in his jaw moved as he chewed and swallowed. "Like you."

She dusted off her fingers. "And how am I like a pizza? Except for the supreme part."

"Bursting with flavor, but probably not good for me."

Kat laughed heartily and folded up her own slice, shoving half of it into her mouth.

"I've never seen a woman with such a ravenous appetite," he remarked.

"I have a screwed-up metabolism," she said around a mouthful of pizza. "My wolf is always in starvation mode."

"Yet you have the same figure as Nadia."

Her eyes flashed up with interest that Prince had noticed her body. It kind of made her want to blush, except Kat hadn't blushed since she was twelve and a boy named Danny had kissed her on a dare. Twelve was much too young for a Shifter girl to be kissing boys, and Kat hadn't done it again until she was twenty-one.

Kat finished her last bite and licked her finger. "My job requires a lot of running and climbing over walls, so I guess I need all the calories I can cram in."

His eyes slid down to her legs and back up again.

"Are you doing what I think you're doing?" she asked. It was a trait Kat was familiar with because she did the same thing in her profession.

"I... I was..."

When color touched his cheeks, she couldn't help but smirk. The stammering was even more adorable.

"I *meant* reading my body language, but I'll let you have an awkward moment of silence to think of an answer."

Prince sighed and continued eating his pizza.

"Did Nadia go out to the club?" Kat set the box on the floor and kicked it out of the way.

He finished his slice in less than four bites and then stretched out his legs. "To meet with a client."

"See, I'm not the only workaholic around here." She licked a few crumbs off her lips. "Thanks for trying the pizza."

He arched a brow and studied her for a moment. Even sitting, Prince was much taller than she was. "I didn't perceive it as a gallant act, but you're welcome."

He's so charming, she thought to herself. Kat leaned forward and began unlacing her boots. "It shows you trust me. Just a little bit."

"Perhaps I was just being polite," he offered.

She glared at him over her shoulder. "Packmasters don't eat food offered from complete strangers just to be polite. Not someone as old as you, who's probably seen firsthand how effective poisons are against an enemy. Ancients aren't polite by nature."

"You can sense I'm an ancient?"

A smile tugged at the corner of her mouth and she pulled off her boots. "You have that stiff look about you. Plus, I see a few wisdom hairs in there."

"Wisdom hairs?"

Kat reached out and plucked one of the rogue silver hairs from his head. He winced and recoiled. She held it in front of his face and tickled his nose with it. "Don't worry, it'll grow back. You might even get three in its place."

He snatched the hair from her fingertips and let it fall to the floor. "That's an old wives' tale."

"Aha! So you've done it. I didn't take you for a man who dyed his hair; you can always spot a dye job a mile away on a guy. I would have never guessed you were a plucker."

He leaned on the armrest and faced her. "And what of *your* artificial color?"

Kat laughed and flipped her hair between her fingers. "This is the real McCoy. Did you think Nadia's hair was naturally blond? She touches up the roots before they're noticeable. She always wanted to be a princess, and I guess she looks like one now."

"You *are* from a royal bloodline," Prince said firmly, clearly aware of her heritage.

The room was dark except for the light emanating from the curio, and it cast shadows along the contours of his face. He was easy on the eyes—a regal nose, slight widow's peak, a strong jaw with dark whiskers just beneath the surface if you looked close enough. Features you wouldn't see on a warrior so much as a king. Despite his age and a few silver hairs, he had a young look about him, seasoned somewhere in his late thirties.

Kat shrugged. "People don't care about the royal bloodline now that we have Councils and the higher authority. Not all the Shifters today know about the old countries that didn't enslave our kind. Most probably don't have a clue that in some places, Shifters once held a lot of power and control, led by royal families. Even if it were common knowledge, I doubt most would care."

"Yes," he agreed, his gaze drifting toward a dark corner. "Years ago, when rumors of Shifter slavery began to surface, it planted a seed with some of the more power-hungry immortals. They coveted our wealth and dominion. Why allow us to flourish when most places were treating us no better than cattle? Our only true magic is shifting to animal form, so many subjugated our kind, forcing wolves to pull sleds, our horses to travel, and our panthers as recreational punishment. I left two places I called home when this insidious mentality began to spread like a plague."

"Must have been a hard life for an alpha, always on the move and starting over."

Boy, did Kat know all about that. She moved so much she practically lived out of a plastic bag more than a suitcase.

"I did what was required to survive. I thought Russia would hold; we had so many in positions of power there." He rested his chin against his fist, swept up in the memories. "Your father was an intelligent man. While he made alliances with other Breeds, he also recruited Shifters into the territory to increase our numbers. We had a strong footing for many years. But times were changing; war was imminent even among the humans. Alex never spoke of me?"

Kat shook her head, remembering how reluctant her father was to discuss the details of his past. Only when he was full of spirits did he recount the glory days before it all went to hell. But when Kat would ask more questions, he'd switch to a lighter topic, saying his princess didn't need to hear such stories of horror and bloodshed. Her father's pain was buried deep, and as much as she'd wanted him to confide in her, it wasn't worth taking the chance that those old memories resurfacing could destroy that man he'd become.

She curled her legs beneath her and turned on her right side to face him. Prince seemed like the kind of man she could talk to— someone who wouldn't hold back, and she liked that about him. "Were you two close?"

"We were like brothers." A rueful smile crossed his face, revealing the same anguished look she'd once seen from her father.

"And what happened that you haven't seen him after all this time?"

A dark look dimmed the light in his eyes. "They imprisoned your father and banished me from my home. They threatened to execute him if I returned. I often wondered if it was an empty threat to keep me out—that perhaps they'd already murdered him long ago on that winter's day."

Kat lowered her gaze, saddened by the hard truth about her father's past. "Why did they treat you differently and let you go?"

"Because, Kat, your father gave up his freedom for mine."

The admission stole her breath.

"Your father was a peacemaker who forged alliances, but I had a reputation for battle that preceded me. One man in the Mage alliance wanted me dead. He knew I would have organized the packs and steered them to war; it wouldn't have been the first time. For reasons I'll never understand, Alex took my place."

A sharp pain lanced through Kat's tender heart when she thought of her father's bravery. "The night he disappeared, he wanted to meet with me. He said he had information on someone I was tracking down at the time. He was like that—always helping me out. I think he was proud of what I did because I was the closest he had to a son. Anyhow, he owned a retreat in the woods no one knew about—a place we used to go fishing and hunting. That's where I was supposed to meet him. When I got there, it had been ransacked, and I haven't heard from him since."

Prince turned toward her and his scent swirled in the air. It was a heady, desirable smell that made her toes curl and her wolf perk up. "Do you think it had to do with the case you were on?"

"That's all I can think of. My father didn't have enemies that I knew of, just a few local Packmasters who didn't get along with him. But that goes with the territory, right?"

"You are correct."

Kat smirked when he didn't get the joke. "Do you ever just say 'yep'?"

He stared, expressionless.

"Okay, maybe not," Kat murmured. Some of the ancients weren't easy to get to loosen up.

"What is the name of the suspect you were chasing?"

Her eyes latched on to his. "I can't tell you that unless you swear an oath to help me search for him."

His mismatched eyes widened and Kat suppressed a grin.

"Sorry, I can't trust just *anyone* with the knowledge I have. I'm sworn to secrecy with the higher authority. The only people I can share intel with are partners. I guess the real question is: how good of friends were you with my father, and how indebted are you to his ultimate sacrifice?"

Prince stood up, his expression cross, hands disappearing into his pockets. "You are a conniving woman."

She crossed her legs nonchalantly. "Some use the word intelligent, but I'll accept that as a compliment."

His eyes shifted down to her foot, watching as she swung it back and forth in a nervous motion. He seemed nicer than the other men Nadia had dated. Most were cocky as hell, and not in a good way. But Prince, he was a different sort of man. Strong, powerful, and over six feet tall, whereas Kat stood at a respectable five-eight, although her boots gave her a nice boost. Prince didn't talk incessantly or try to hit on her. *He must worship Nadia.*

"Will you accept my second-in-command to help you out?"

She put both feet on the floor and stood up, hands on her hips. "Absolutely not. You want to send a beta to do an alpha's job?"

Prince removed his hands from his pockets and his jaw set.

"Is that how much my father meant to you?" Kat continued, rocking on her heels and giving him a somber look. This time she wasn't putting on an act but was genuinely disappointed that a man who had bonded with her father as a brother would pawn off the task of searching for him.

"Very well. But if we hit a stumbling block, then I'll have to bow out. I have obligations as a Packmaster."

"I'm sure you have a capable second-in-command who can lead your pack temporarily." She snatched his tie and gave it a light tug. "Come on, Charming."

He stepped back, his brows drawing together. "My name is Prince."

He's so adorable, she thought. "I can't go around calling you Prince, so Charming will have to do. It has a nice ring to it."

"So does *sire*."

Kat stepped forward and stood on her tiptoes. "I'm not one of your subjects."

His breath heated her face and made her tingle in all the wrong places. Wrong, because this was Nadia's territory.

Kat stepped back and twirled his tie before letting go. "Do you normally dress to the nines for a date?"

"I like to make an impression."

When she yanked on her boots, she peered over her shoulder and caught him looking at her ass. Yep. When you stripped away money and rank, all men wanted the same things.

Kat stood up so quickly that her hair flipped over her head. She gave it a nice pat down and then tapped the toe of her boot on the floor. "Coming?"

"*Now?*" he asked, his voice flustered.

"Yep. I tracked this bozo all the way from Shreveport, and my contact gave me a location where he hangs out. I figure that's a good place to start. He's still classified as an outlaw, which means I can bring him back dead or alive. I'd rather bring him back alive so I can question him. Plus, I don't like hauling bodies in the trunk of my car, especially in the South. The state troopers out here just love to pull you over and search your vehicle."

"And what makes you so certain this is the same man who took your father?"

Kat switched off the curio and stumbled over a rug in the darkness. She caught herself on the wall before taking a spill. "Because he's the guy my father wanted to talk to me about—the one I was tracking all those years ago. The bounty is still open, and I'm going to collect."

Kat whirled around and headed toward the front door, forgetting about the small step into the hall. She stumbled forward and this time fell on her face.

"Dammit!"

Prince rushed to her side and put his hands on her back. "Are you injured?"

"Only my pride," she murmured against the smooth floor, grateful Nadia was a neat freak and cleaned it every day.

"Perhaps you've had too much wine."

Kat sprang to her feet. "Get used to it, Charming. I barely had a few sips, so I'm not even tipsy. I just happen to have a habit of tripping over things—usually those things being my own two feet. I'm better when I'm running full speed. Something about the slow pace of a stroll makes my limbs forget how to function. So do me a favor and don't make a big deal about it when I fall down in public."

"You mean *if* you fall."

She laughed and pulled a small set of keys from her pocket. "There are no ifs about it. I'm a girl who falls head over heels."

CHAPTER 4

P RINCE FELT A PANG OF guilt for leaving Nadia's apartment without telling her, but only for a fleeting moment. After all, she'd left him alone with her sister to test how interested he was in pursuing her and no one else, treating Prince more like a lapdog than an alpha wolf. Instead of sending her a message on the phone, he left a handwritten note on her dining table explaining that he'd gone out with Kat for a few drinks.

And he intentionally wrote Kat instead of Katarina. Prince enjoyed the abbreviated name. She intrigued him, and he'd sensed early on that both Kat and Nadia were alpha females.

In the Shifter world, children were either born an alpha or not, and usually it was the firstborn. Anyone could have strong leadership skills, but alphas possessed more magic within them, more control over their animal than the others. That power resonated in their voice, their presence, and especially in their wolf. Only an alpha could become a Packmaster and lead a pack to success; anyone else was doomed to failure. Alpha females were especially desirable to Packmasters, and although it wasn't mandatory that they mate with one, alpha females produced stouthearted children and commanded a pack like no other.

And yet even more curious was that Kat's magic was a little stronger than her sister's. Kat's power flashed while Nadia's only pulsed.

When they arrived at the club, Prince watched with curiosity as Kat reached into the backseat and retrieved a pair of black-and-white sneakers. She yanked off her boots and tossed them on the floor. He never knew what to expect with this woman.

Prince cleared his throat.

"What? I love my Chucks," she said unapologetically, lacing them up. "Besides, the boots kill my feet on a chase. Last time, I got blisters the size of cantaloupes. I know, I know. It clashes with my leather pants, but I don't have any options since I left town in a hurry. My good running shoes are sitting in a motel room in Shreveport." Kat opened the visor mirror and raked her fingers through her hair. "I really need to start carrying an extra set of clothes in the car."

"The man we're looking for—what's his name?"

"The bartender said his name is Henry, but when I accepted the job to hunt him down years ago, the name they gave me was Vlad Romanov."

Prince's blood ran cold. "Then we're dealing with a Mage."

Her eyes widened. "How did you know?"

He scanned her outfit, his heart ticking a little faster. "You said you carry a stunner?"

When Kat began to lift her shirt, he averted his eyes to the dark parking lot.

She laughed and tapped his arm. "I'm not coming on to you, Charming. I wear short shirts for easy access. Wait, that sounded wrong," she murmured. "I wear a harness around my chest. It was custom made since boobs get in the way."

Her candor made his face flush, and he tried to give her a scolding glance. Tried and failed.

Kat smiled fiendishly, straightening her blouse. "Sorry. Sometimes I'm a little too frank, but you shouldn't be so wooden about language. It's the only way I can get in with some of the guys who hang out at the bar. They don't give information to girls with Russian accents who speak prim and proper, now do they? Anyhow, the knife is tucked on my left side, but the strap goes over my shoulder and around my chest and has a lot of small compartments— including a clip to hold handcuffs. My old one was pretty basic and the holster sat in the center of my chest, but that hurt too much and was harder to conceal when wearing low-cut shirts."

Prince kept imagining her without a shirt, the holster strapped tight against her left breast, the feel of her leather pants as she stretched across his lap… He shifted in his seat. "How did you find Vlad after all these years?"

"He walked into a bar where I was hot on the trail of an arms dealer—the kind who specializes in stunners and rare weaponry. I guess the higher authority got sick of this scuzzball when one of his weapons killed a hotshot Mage. Anyhow, I was having a drink in the bar, and Vlad walked right in and sat beside me. I didn't recognize him at first because the last time I'd seen him was twenty years ago, but the longer I stared at him in the mirror, the more familiar he seemed. He looks the same, except he has a lot of whiskers, like he's trying to grow a pathetic excuse for a beard. Same cloudy eyes, blondish hair that's real short to his head, same mean face, like Russian KGB."

Prince glanced at her body again, wondering if handcuffs were part of her master plan. "Cuffs won't hold a Mage."

Kat waggled her brows. "Mine will. You'd be surprised what kind of metals are out there. That's why these aren't clunky. I don't carry them with me all the time—not unless I'm on the hunt. These will make him as dangerous as a butterfly," she said, flapping her hands comically. "I just need to get close enough to put the knife in his chest before I haul him off."

Prince laughed and opened his door. "I sense this evening will not be uneventful."

"Nope! A night with me is never a bore."

The young couple standing in front of the club, tongues down each other's throats, led Prince to believe this wasn't the type of Breed establishment he'd normally be seen in. He frequented a few clubs and sometimes went to Howlers, a Shifter bar with a relaxed atmosphere where he could be among his own kind. Prince didn't mind the company of most Breeds, but he could never trust a Mage.

Possessive instincts overwhelmed him when they entered the bar and two Vampires leered at Kat with their onyx eyes. She didn't possess the same delicate mannerisms as her sister, nor did she wear short skirts that showed off her legs, but she garnered attention just the same with her sultry strut and self-assured way of settling her eyes on a man.

Prince eased up next to her and put his arm around her shoulder.

Kat nudged it off. "Don't do that, Charming. People will think we're an item."

"That's my intent. Then maybe they'll cease giving you proprietary looks."

Kat coughed and waved a cloud of smoke away as they moved toward a dark area. "Say what you will, but this body is what gets people talking to me."

He clenched his fists, his knuckles whitening. "And you find this acceptable behavior?"

"You don't think Nadia uses her body to attract clients?" They stopped by a wall, and she ran her finger down his silk tie. "And what about you and your expensive suits and imported cologne? Not to mention that sexy ponytail thing you've got going on. You don't think that gets people's attention a little more than say... *that* guy?" She jerked her thumb toward a man in a blue flannel shirt, five buttons brazenly undone to reveal a thick bed of chest hair.

Prince lowered his eyes to meet hers. "Isn't your job dangerous enough?"

When her lips tightened, he realized he'd offended her.

"I hope you're not one of those guys who think a woman gets what she deserves because of what she's wearing. A supremely stupid man made up that logic to blame women for his lack of control. I've locked up a lot of men in my time, and you wouldn't believe the excuses I've heard. For example, if I strip down naked in this bar, then every man and woman has the right to look at me because... well, there I am. Kind of hard not to notice. But not one damn person has the right to touch me."

"I trust you don't intend to test that theory."

Her eyes narrowed, dark lashes obscuring her brown eyes. "I'm shy, so that's not on the agenda. My belly button is the only magic show you're getting tonight."

Odd. Nadia had no trouble showing off her fit body, and yet her identical twin struggled with self-image?

Kat suddenly sneezed and rubbed her nose. "Look, I know how to take care of myself. If I want to wear tight leather pants to get an informant to let his guard down and give me information, then that's a sacrifice I'll readily make." She gasped, on the verge of sneezing, and then let out a sigh. "Sometimes I wish human laws applied to Breed establishments."

He tilted his head to the side, startled by the sudden change in topic. "They're not aware we exist, so we don't have to follow their laws. Not as long as we keep them out of our clubs."

She sneezed again, and it was high-pitched and quite pleasing to watch. "Well, I've always been a supporter of their smoking ban. Some of these immortals puff like a chimney, and it does a number on my allergies."

Prince wiped a drop of sweat off his forehead, wishing he'd left his suit jacket in the car. "Shifters aren't afflicted with allergies."

She rubbed her nose. "Yeah? Well, I'm a sensitive girl. Say, why don't you dash over to the bar and grab me a bottle of beer so we blend in? Don't get me any of the fancy-pants stuff."

"What is your preferred brand?"

She snapped her fingers and briefly closed her eyes. "Ohh, 'Fire and Rain.' I *love* this song." She quietly sang a few lines before she turned her attention back to the bar. "Let's not make this complicated. Just point at one of the green bottles."

Prince headed toward the bar and paid for a bottle, hoping his selection would please Kat. He even compared brands and chose the most expensive. Strange that he'd want to please her when they'd only just met. Prince felt comfortable in her presence, as if they'd known each other for years. The only other person he'd ever felt that same connection to was Alex.

It didn't make sense, because he had more in common with her sister. Who else was more suited to be his mate than Nadia? Sophisticated, enchanting, eloquent…

"Your zipper's down," Kat said brightly, snatching the beer from his hand and guzzling it.

Startled, he looked down and—to his horror—realized she was right. Discreetly, he turned away from the room and maneuvered his hand downward before anyone noticed.

Kat suddenly reached out and zipped him up. His eyes widened at her brazen move, and she grinned when the high-pitched sound caught the attention of a woman sitting at a nearby table.

"Don't you have any sense of decency?" he whispered.

She glanced around the bar. "Only on Mondays. Wait, there he is. I'd recognize those jowls anywhere." She nudged Prince and turned him to face the back of the room. "Over to the left near the woman in red. You can't miss her; she stands out like a stuck pig in a cotton factory. Who needs to dress like *that?* Some women display their breasts like they're melons at a farmer's market."

"Let's say hello," he said, pushing off the wall and centering his eyes on Vlad.

"Wait!" she whispered urgently. "You'll spook him."

"And your plan was to tackle him on the way to the men's room?" he asked with derision as they moved toward the table. All Prince could think about was wrapping his hands around Vlad's throat and squeezing until the life pulsed out of him.

Kat suddenly plopped down in the chair directly behind Vlad. She crossed her legs, downed her beer, and bored a hole in the back of his skull with her heated gaze. Prince continued walking without questioning her actions.

The music switched to another song when he pulled the chair out and sat across from the old Mage. When Vlad lifted his head from his glass of vodka, his glazed eyes settled on Prince for a few moments before a flicker of recognition sparked in them.

"Well, well. If it isn't *Prince.* Vanquished two centuries ago and crawling back to civilization like a reptile emerging from a swamp," Vlad said in a heavy Russian accent.

"Banished, not vanquished," Prince stated flatly. "And how have the years treated you? Did you enjoy the spoils of war? Money and power can be fleeting for those who don't know how to conserve."

Vlad took another drink and slammed the glass down, raising his stony eyes to Prince. He was a hard-looking man with a weathered face and blond hair that seemed half a shade away from white. His eyes were the color of slate, and when he smiled, he showed more gum than teeth.

"You look different. I wouldn't have recognized you if not for those devil eyes," Vlad said. "They should have burned you as a witch centuries ago. One less Shifter infesting the world." He lifted his glass, gave it a swirl, and then polished it off.

Prince maintained his composure. "Now that humans have mastered electricity, your Mage gifts seem far less impressive. No better than a battery."

Vlad flashed him a hostile look. He was not only an immortal, but had the ability to manipulate energy, releasing it through his hands as a weapon to any non-Mage. Prince had built up a tolerance to the energy blasts over the years because of his alpha magic, so one powerful shock wouldn't knock him unconscious. It gave him enough time to stay in the fight until he could bind their hands, unless he was in wolf form, in which case his wolf would tear apart their limbs, rendering them useless long enough for him to kill the Mage before they could heal. A Mage could flash—running at incredible speeds for short periods of time, so it was crucial to take them down as soon as you were within reach.

Prince removed his jacket and placed it over the back of the chair next to him. "Tell me, Vlad, what became of Alexei Kozlov?"

Instead of thinking for a moment with his gaze adrift as most men do when asked a question that requires them to reflect back a few hundred years, Vlad gave him a lopsided grin and sat back in his chair, flicking his near-empty glass away.

"I sometimes wish I hadn't taken his offer. It would have been worth turning down his fortune to see you rot in a Russian Breed jail. It's nothing like the air-conditioned rooms they have now. We served them gruel, if they were lucky. Wolves were tied to sleds in winter to get the men around, and inside the jails they were shackled and beaten. I felt no remorse for someone who gave up his freedom for yours. That showed me what a weak and stupid man he was."

Prince quelled his anger, centering his eyes on Vlad, uncertain of what rare Mage gifts he might have—ones they often kept concealed. Some could sense emotions, others jumped long distances, and every Mage had at least one rare gift that could give them the advantage in a fight.

Prince leaned forward. "What happened to Alexei?"

Vlad sniffed indifferently. "Once we drove the Shifters out, we had all the power. But soon the humans who knew of our existence became afraid and rose up against us. We tried to get the situation under control, but they threatened to expose us to the public and drive us to extinction. I'm not afraid of humans; they're weak. But the leaders didn't think we could win a war without numbers. Guards were ordered to kill the prisoners before evacuating, but Alexei was one of six wolves given a temporary exception. They were to transport a general across the border and return, but when they did, they were short a man. Alexei had escaped." Vlad rubbed the whiskers on his jaw.

"Why so disappointed? Alexei did nothing but make you a wealthy man."

"He also paid off a general to set him free."

Prince smiled with satisfaction, realizing Alex hadn't given all his fortune to Vlad but had also hidden some. "Clever."

"Stupid. He could have paid me off a long time ago to set him free. Instead, he chose to rot in jail like the cowardly mongrel he is."

A sharp blade appeared at Vlad's throat, and Kat gripped his jaw with her left arm. "You know what's stupid? That some idiot Creator out there deemed you worthy of immortality. That makes about as much sense as tits on a bull."

Prince's lip twitched at her colorful expression.

Kat wrinkled her nose. "Clearly I've spent too much time down South," she said to Prince, annoyed.

"Who's your friend?" Vlad asked Prince, not showing any signs of intimidation even though he had a blade pressing at his jugular.

Prince considered how to answer, but Kat took the honors.

"I'm the firstborn daughter to Alexei Kozlov." Rivulets of blood trickled down Vlad's neck. "Now tell me where he is," she growled, a cascade of her hair falling forward and concealing half his face.

"Do you think your little dagger frightens me?"

"How attached are you to your head, Dracula?"

Vlad scowled. "Don't call me that. I'm *not* a Vampire."

Prince pulled out the chair on his right and coaxed her to sit with a wave of his hand. Kat was seething with anger and had every right. In another lifetime, Prince would have challenged a man who insulted him or someone he respected. But these were different times where men didn't settle disputes with swords. Killing an outlaw wouldn't have been a crime so much as committing the act in a Breed establishment. Prince had to carefully choose his battles or else he risked losing his pack. Kat, on the other hand, didn't seem to have anything to lose.

"Kat, have a seat." Prince gave her an intense look, radiating alpha power in the resonance of his voice.

Reluctantly, she pulled the dagger away and tucked it back in the holster beneath her shirt. When Kat turned to sit, she stumbled on her shoelace and almost missed the chair. She quickly gripped the edge of the table and sat up straight, her eyes locked on Vlad.

"Where's my father?"

Vlad picked up the wet napkin from beneath his glass and used it to wipe the blood droplets from his neck. "What makes you think I know where your father is?"

"Twenty years ago, you were my pet project. Because of your Russian name, I figured my father might have heard of you. As it turns out, I was right. On the night he asked to speak to me privately, he went missing. Didn't just go missing, but someone ransacked his cabin in the process. Exactly what were you looking for?"

Vlad lifted his empty glass and tasted the last drops from the bottom. "You are mistaken."

"Pussy."

With lightning speed, Vlad rose up and slammed the glass to the floor. Prince stood up and flipped the table over when he saw blue light trickling from Vlad's fingertips.

Before Vlad could put his energy-soaked hands on Kat, she shifted into her wolf. Her dense fur was the color of black velvet, her body built for speed. She circled behind Vlad and pounced onto his back, sinking her sharp canines into his fleshy neck.

"Ah! Get it off!" he shouted, crashing to the floor.

Prince stepped on Vlad's right hand to keep him from harming Kat's wolf, although he had no control over the other arm. "You dare attack a female?" he roared.

Vlad grimaced. "That's no female; that's the devil incarnate." He grunted through clenched teeth. "I see savagery is still the way of the Shifter."

A few people nearby stood up but chose not to intervene since it hadn't escalated.

However, if Kat's wolf took off Vlad's head, then the bar might erupt in chaos. She wasn't going to shift back on her own, so Prince decided to force her.

He removed his jacket and knelt down, placing his hand on her wolf's neck. "*Shift.*"

In a fluid movement, the wolf gracefully changed to human form. Despite the fact that a beautiful woman was naked in the middle of a club, the Shifters went back to their drinks, chuckling about the scuffle. It was the other Breeds that looked on with lust in their eyes. Kat's wavy black hair spread down her back like a mane, although not quite long enough to cover the dip of her spine and the round curve of her backside.

"Dammit, Charming. I told you I'm *shy!*"

A flannel shirt flew out of nowhere and landed on her back. "Put that on, sugar. Unless you want to start a war in here," the hairy-chested man said. He sat back down, his beer gut hanging over the top of his tight jeans.

Still straddling the bleeding Mage, Kat slipped into the flannel shirt and buttoned it up. "If you *ever* come at me like that again, Count Chocula, you'll be lucky to walk away with two testicles." She smacked him on the back of the head and stood up, straightening her long shirt.

Despite shifting, the holster for her dagger remained strapped to her body. It was customized to also fit her wolf, so it hadn't come off during the shift.

Vlad sat up, gripping the back of his bloody neck. "You're a crazy bitch if you think I'm going to tell you anything."

Kat finished slipping on her sneakers and started to reach into her shirt, but it was buttoned up and far too long. She knitted her brows and looked down, undoing the top buttons so she could retrieve something from her harness beneath. "I'm also a bounty hunter, and I'm taking you in."

Vlad lunged at her with his hands out, and Kat's eyes went wide when she pulled her hand out with a set of cuffs, which fell to the floor. Prince lunged between them and took the brunt of the hit, a powerful surge of energy slamming into his chest. It tightened every muscle in his body, and he fell backward with Kat beneath him.

She groaned weakly. "I hate it when they do that," she mumbled. "Charming?"

Prince cursed under his breath when he saw Vlad flash out of sight. "Yes?"

"Normally I wouldn't complain about a hot guy with a ponytail lying on top of me while I'm half-naked, but I'm suffocating."

He forced himself up, rolling off Kat as every muscle in his body screamed back to life. Her plaid shirt was long enough to cover her womanhood, but as Prince looked down at Kat lying at his feet, wearing only her sneakers and another man's shirt, all he could think about was kissing her.

CHAPTER 5

"**D**ON'T EVER DO THAT AGAIN." Kat stewed in the driver's seat of her car, irritated that Prince had made her shift in front of everyone. "My wolf had everything under control. She knows better than to kill the man I'm after. Well, except for that one time in Memphis. But he had it coming."

"Have you forgotten it's against the rules to shift in a bar?" he asked, rolling his window halfway down. The air blew in, but his hair was so tightly bound that it didn't move.

Unlike hers, which swirled around the car like silken whips.

"What are they going to do, blacklist me? It wouldn't be the first time I've been kicked out of a bar, and it sure won't be the last. If you had spent less time worrying about rules, we'd have Vlad in the trunk of my car where he belongs."

"He won't get far," Prince said matter-of-factly, wiping at something on his trousers.

Kat didn't like opportunities to slide by, and she glowered. "What makes you so sure he won't skip town?"

"If he made a sudden trip to Austin, then it's for a reason. Men like him don't hide; they conspire. He's less concerned about getting caught than you think."

Kat hit the steering wheel with her fist. "Dammit! I *had* him. It's taken me twenty years to catch up with this guy, and I let him slip through my fingers. This isn't just a job, Charming."

"We'll find him."

"Not if he goes into hiding."

When Prince rolled up his window, the quiet hum of the road beneath the tires became soothing.

Prince gently touched her arm. "I meant your father."

Her lip trembled, and she briefly looked out her window so he wouldn't notice. That's when she spotted Nadia's car pulling into the parking garage of her complex.

Swell.

When he let go of her arm, she immediately felt his absence. Maybe it was because he was the only person who'd ever shown compassion for the pain of losing her father. Even Nadia had never offered a hug—she'd simply shut down, deciding they'd been abandoned by *both* parents. Kat had no one else to turn to, no one to offer her a consoling touch or a kind word. Worst of all, she was too embarrassed—too proud—to ask Prince to continue touching her a little longer.

She parked the car near a large pear tree, the dull glow of a streetlamp illuminating the hood. Her Mustang was bright yellow with a black racing stripe down the center. People made jokes about it, but when Kat was on the run in a crowded parking lot, she didn't have any problem distinguishing her vehicle from the rest.

"I can't believe I left my pants at the bar."

They had been in such a rush to leave that she'd not only left her clothes behind, but Prince had left his suit jacket draped over the back of his chair, which was probably toppled over.

"I'm sure your sister will offer something that will fit," he suggested, a smile ghosting his lips.

Kat all but snarled at him. "I'm sure you find that really amusing since we're identical, but there's no way in Hades I'm putting on one of her white pantsuits to chase outlaws. Aside from that, I can bet you she's not about to lend me anything. I guess I'll have to continue this investigation pantless."

When his eyes dragged down to her bare legs, it sent an unexpected lick of heat through her body.

His tongue swiped his bottom lip, and he dodged her gaze. "Would nothing of hers meet your approval?"

She pulled the keys out of the ignition and played with the silver ring. "I'm a jeans and T-shirt kind of girl. I like cozy, and nothing that woman owns is cozy. All she has in her den of iniquity are outfits that are tight, white, and full of buttons, straps, or laces. I don't expect you to understand this because first off, you're a man. Secondly, you dress like a billionaire on his way to a yacht to get laid by the peanut butter heiress."

Prince burst out laughing and shielded his eyes. His unfettered emotions were an attractive quality, but he rarely let out a spontaneous laugh, and she was curious why he seemed embarrassed by it.

"You have a unique way of speaking, Kat. I don't think I could tire of listening to you."

"I can't tell whether you're joking or serious, but let's just say that most men can only handle me in small doses."

She got out of the car and slammed the door, heading toward Nadia's urban apartments. As they moved through the main door, Prince not only held it open for her but placed the flat of his hand on her back and kept pace with her. He was courteous, and that was a big deal given most men didn't bother with all the civilities with a bounty hunter.

Get it together, Kat, she thought to herself. *Getting cozy with your sister's boyfriend? Not cool.*

Yet during the elevator ride up, Kat kept stealing glimpses of her Charming. When he loosened his grey tie and rolled up his sleeves, her eyes gobbled up the strong cords of muscle along his forearms. He wasn't pale either; it looked like the sun had kissed his skin in worship. Beneath all those layers of Armani was an alpha who took care of his body. Maybe these newfound feelings were from exhaustion after a long day that had ended with her naked on the back of an outlaw, or maybe it was that extra slice of pizza she'd had earlier, but visions of Prince lifting her off the ground and kissing her hard infiltrated her thoughts. Especially given she wasn't wearing pants, let alone panties, and all it would take was unfastening his zipper and...

The elevator bell chimed and the doors opened.

Nadia was standing in front of them with a piece of paper between two fingers. "Did you show my guest a good time?" she asked Kat. Then her eyes journeyed downward and noticed the lack of clothing. "Never mind. Up to your usual mischief." She pivoted around, her heels clicking on the hard floor as she made her way inside the apartment.

Kat followed behind and took a deep breath, still smelling the remnants of pizza, which overpowered the quail. She pulled a can of soda from the vegetable drawer in the fridge, her hiding spot for fizzy drinks since Nadia never looked down there. After cracking it open and sucking off the foam, she went into the living room and plopped down on the couch.

Prince lingered in the lit hall to Kat's left, speaking privately with Nadia. Kat watched the subtle nuances of their body language, wondering what they were whispering about.

When Nadia stepped closer to him and brushed her hand down his arm, Kat bit the edge of her soda can. Nadia could choose from any man she wanted, and yet she wanted none of them. Kat didn't bother with the chase since most men weren't going to warm up to mating with a bounty hunter anyhow.

Men were sexually attracted to Kat, and that was about as far as it went. Most couldn't relate to a woman who had a knife strapped to her chest, and few cared what she had to say. It wasn't so bad. After they slipped out in the middle of the night, Kat could finally have the bed to herself and kick off the covers. It meant she didn't have to wake up early and cook someone breakfast, because she liked sleeping in and nibbling on leftovers from the night before. It meant not having to hear someone complain that she worked too much.

But it also meant being lonely at night. Sometimes she'd lie in bed, thinking how nice it would be to curl up with someone. Not just anyone, but a man she could actually hold a conversation with. Eventually Kat would roll over and start thinking about her next case, because dwelling on a life she couldn't have was poisonous. All that "grass is greener" thinking gets people into trouble. It was why her mother had left, and Kat didn't want to become a woman who was never satisfied with her life.

Prince and Nadia continued speaking in low voices, and Kat admired his casual stance. His pants had a stain, his shirt was wrinkled, sleeves rolled up, tie loose, and yet he carried himself like a man to be reckoned with. Nadia leaned forward in a way that signaled she was going for some tongue action. Kat looked away and slurped on her soda, wishing she could teleport herself to a five-star hotel where they had room service. When the murmurs quieted and she heard the sound of lips touching, she stole a quick glance.

Prince kissed Nadia's cheek near the corner of her mouth, but Nadia was a shark when it came to making out. Now that she smelled blood in the water, she was going to circle her prey until she got what she wanted. Nadia was a first-date kisser because she said that a man's tongue revealed what kind of lover he was.

It didn't look like she was getting the scoop on Prince's prowess in bed tonight. Kat smiled wide in victory.

When Prince glanced over his right shoulder and looked right at her, she almost dropped her soda.

"Good night, Kat. It was a memorable evening."

"Cheers," she said, holding up her drink in the dark room.

Memorable, she pondered. *Not enchanting, and definitely not exciting. Well, I'll never see* him *again.* Which was a shame. Vlad was going to be impossible to hunt down now that she'd scared him away from his regular hangout. Prince knew Vlad and could probably help, but guys like him didn't like to get mixed up in dangerous drama like this. Especially with a girl like Kat. The worst part? She actually liked his company.

Maybe too much.

Nadia locked the door and joined Kat in the living room, kicking off her heels and running her hands through her silky blond hair. "Should I be concerned you weren't wearing pants with my date?"

"Why do you hate me?"

Nadia sat down to Kat's left, her voice weary. "I don't hate you, Katarina. I just don't understand you."

Kat could sense the hurt in her voice, and it had to do with why they were so different. "Papa spent more time with me, but not because he loved me more. He just didn't know what to do with a little girl who loved tea parties and dresses. He liked to hunt, fish, and shoot guns."

"And you did those things to please him?" She twisted her hair back and clasped her hands behind her head.

"No. I wouldn't do something I don't enjoy. This is just who I am. Plus, I never really liked tea. Only your invisible friends were allowed to sit at the table."

"My friends aren't invisible anymore, and I have a life. One you seem to disrupt every chance you get. I don't mind the visits, darling, but you have too much chaos in your suitcase. There are other jobs. I could find you something here if you want to live close to me."

"I like what I do," Kat said, hiding her annoyance. "Someone has to put away the bad guys so you don't have to look over your shoulder as often."

"How long will you be staying this time?"

"Until I find Papa."

Nadia sighed and lowered her arms. "That again. He's gone, Katarina. Like our mother."

"She left us. Someone *took* Papa. And… well, Prince wants to help me." Kat innocently sipped her soda.

"Oh, no he isn't!" Nadia burst out, quickly turning to face Kat. "You're very clever at talking people into things, but Prince is a high-ranking Packmaster in this territory, if not the highest. You could jeopardize his standing with the Council if he gets into trouble."

Kat set her can of soda on the floor and sat up. "Don't you see? He's the only one who can help. He knew our father, and he knows this guy. Papa didn't have many close friends that I know about, and I get the feeling these two were tight."

"I won't have it," Nadia continued, standing up and pacing the floor. "This is where I draw the line."

Kat swung her legs onto the sofa and crossed them at the ankle. "No need to get your panties in a bunch. After tonight, he probably won't come within a five-mile radius of me. I pulled a knife, shifted in a bar, ruined his suit… the usual."

"*Charming.*"

That roused a subtle smile on Kat's face when she thought of how the word "charming" held a different meaning now. It was her pet name for Prince, and Kat was fond of nicknames.

"So, how long have you two been seeing each other?"

Nadia reached behind her curio and switched on the light so she could admire the figurines. Each one had its place, and Kat knew this because she'd once rearranged them to see if Nadia would notice.

"This was our first date."

Kat grimaced. "Oops. I'm sorry. Hopefully I didn't scare him off. I thought you two were a thing."

"We'll see," she replied with an air of confidence. "He has all the right qualifications, but I'm not sure if I'm ready to join a pack for any man, even a Packmaster."

Kat snorted. "You'd have to keep a whole lot of packmates in line."

Nadia ran her finger along the glass cabinet and checked it for dust. "His mansion seems quiet enough. I didn't get the impression he leads a rambunctious pack."

"Mansion? Wow. He really *is* loaded. Sounds like a match made in heaven."

"Do you think I require a man's money? I have my own."

Kat curled up on her right side, having heard this song and dance before. "You're a hoarder, Nads. You make more money than most people I know, and all you do is buy pretty dresses and pricey cheese. And those figurines."

"Money is security."

Kat yawned, feeling the pull of sleep. "The only security in this world is family. Money comes and goes. You make such a big deal about it, but what's it really done for you? I'm just as happy as you are."

Nadia crossed the room and lingered by the entrance to the hall that led to her bedroom. "Don't pretend money holds no value when you earn a sizable income. Perhaps you should learn to hold on to it."

"Of course it's important, but why not use it to help others? Anyhow, I'm saving up for a big house in the woods someday with a lot of land. Someplace private where I can hunt, fish, and let my wolf run all she wants without having to wake up naked in the parking lot of a Burger King. I haven't figured out where I want to live yet, but if you want to know the truth, I don't work for money. It comes with the job, but I love what I do. I sleep at night knowing that each asshole I lock up means one less person in the world will be hurt by them. Even if the higher authority quit offering rewards, I don't know if I could stop."

Nadia drifted into the hall near the edge of the wall. "Would you like to borrow some panties?"

"Negative. And I shouldn't have to explain why," Kat murmured against the couch pillow. God, how she hated this predicament of not having clothes or money. She preferred cash so no one could lift her wallet and discover her identity, and that wallet was sitting next to a bag of chocolate-covered almonds on her coffee table.

Nadia switched off the hall light. "Well, good night. I'd bring you a blanket to cover up with, but you'll just kick it onto the floor."

"Sis?"

"Yes?"

"Can you put the pizza in the fridge for tomorrow?"

Her voice grew distant. "It's too old to enjoy."

Kat's eyes closed and she mumbled, "It's perfect."

As soon as Prince arrived at his mansion, he ascended the curved staircase to his study and closed the door. It was a quaint room with a mahogany desk to the right—a green banker's lamp casting a warm glow. The entire wall in front of the door was a bookshelf filled with ancient books in six different languages. The two green chairs to the left were rarely used; Prince never invited anyone to join him in this room, and he preferred sitting at his desk where he could work on his laptop.

He took a seat in his leather chair and switched on the computer. He had direct access to a secure database only a select few Packmasters were privy to. It stored information the Council had collected on troublesome Shifters as well as criminal records.

Prince hadn't thought of Vlad Romanov in decades. The problem with living an extended lifespan was that it was inevitable you'd run into familiar faces from the past. Humans like to use the expression that it's a small world, but for Breed, it was infinitely smaller.

He replayed the scene in his mind several times of the Mage thrusting his energy-soaked hands at Kat. Prince should have moved faster; he should have known Vlad would create a diversion and flee the scene. Had Prince reacted a fraction of a second sooner, Kat wouldn't have been hurt at all. A man putting his hands on a woman incited a wave of rage that rippled through him like a tide.

And for that, Vlad would pay.

Then his mind drifted back to Kat. She was so different from Nadia, whose blond locks had first captured his attention. Yet the dark and deliberate nature of Kat's hair made his heart quicken. Whenever she took a deep breath, he noticed her collarbone. It seemed like such an odd thing to focus on, but finding traits that made her different from her twin had become a silent game. The commanding way she threw her shoulders back and cocked her hips to the side when speaking. The confident tone in her voice, her assertive gaze, the level of control. Those qualities beguiled his wolf, making him pace restlessly in her presence—something his wolf had never done for another female. Even her own wolf possessed that same inherent strength by dominating that Mage and making him submit.

Kat's insults were thinly veiled. She judged him because of his wealth and tidy appearance. Yet she had also made references to his long hair on two occasions, once using the word "sexy" to describe it. Prince reached back and pulled the band from his hair, shaking it loose around his shoulders, wondering what Kat would think of it unbound. His long hair connected him to his past and allowed him to see his former self reflecting back at him in the mirror. In that reflection, he also caught glimpses of his father.

Prince became drunk with thoughts of Kat, and for the first time in centuries, he coveted. Wanted to taste her lips, feel her body beneath his, and run with her wolf. Prince shifted in his chair, realizing he'd become thick with arousal. These ungovernable thoughts would consume him if he didn't get control of them. Despite Kat possessing the purity he'd long sought for in a mate, he couldn't afford to have tender feelings for such a woman. A bounty hunter who carried a knife and lived like a nomad—she was completely wrong for him, so he steered his thoughts away.

"Vlad Romanov," he said quietly, staring at the computer screen. "Born in 1721, emigrated from Russia, wanted for slave trafficking."

Sadly, that sort of depravity still went on in the underworld—outside the city limits of most major cities and beyond the reach of the Councils. A sparse few ancient immortals held fast to the old world when they had once lived like kings, using Shifters to do their bidding. Vlad had made a career kidnapping and selling men, women, and children for profit. The file included his last known location and listed Kat as the assigned bounty hunter. Twenty years had passed, but it was still common knowledge that the higher authority never closed a case on an outlaw until they were captured or killed. That's why most criminals kept a low profile and avoided reaching outlaw status.

"Where does a man like you hide?" he asked himself, leaning back in his chair, the leather creaking. "And what brings you to Austin?"

Southern states had more land, but they were regulated by the Councils, and an outlaw wouldn't be able to claim territory unless he did so illegally. It would be easier for his crimes to go unnoticed in a populous city. If Vlad was still selling on the black market, then he might be in town for business. There wasn't a main site like eBay to do this kind of trading, but men who purchased Shifters went through a seller or middleman who would give them private access to his site. After providing their criteria, they sat back and waited for a match.

Prince sent a quick message to an associate who worked undercover with a list of local names to research. Maybe Vlad was in town hunting his next victim.

He closed the laptop and stood up, stretching out the stiff muscles in his back before loosening his slim tie and tossing it onto his desk. As tired as he was, he still felt charged from the events of the evening. He strolled across the hallway to his bedroom while unbuttoning his shirt.

Once inside, he draped the shirt over a chair and removed his leather shoes and black socks. Prince stood before a cheval mirror, his reflection encased in an espresso frame. With his hair loose, he remembered himself as a great leader from centuries ago. Frock coat, gloves, and suspenders to hold up his trousers. Fashion divided the rich and poor in earlier times, and Shifters lived somewhere in the middle. He had always appreciated a good suit; it made him feel elevated amongst others.

Prince was born in Imereti in the thirteen hundreds, firstborn to nomadic parents who had claimed land to establish a pack. They were of the purest blood, and Shifters gravitated toward them. His father had dreams of living a peaceful existence in a farming community, so he started a family in hopes of settling down. But in those times no one could escape war. Immortals were fighting for power, and Shifters were fighting for survival.

Prince unlatched his black belt, pulled it away from his pants, and tossed it to the floor. When he grasped the tab of his zipper, he thought of Kat and a smile touched his lips. Whether it was Prince's open zipper or stumbling over her laces, she didn't dwell on other people's opinions. He usually preferred sophisticated women, ones who trembled with anticipation when he unfastened their corsets, but these women were rarities in the modern world. And here he was, faced with two identical women on the opposite ends of the spectrum. One who represented the ideal woman he revered and who matched his personality, and the other who ensnared his thoughts and heated his blood in a way no woman ever had.

Prince was a man of restraint, one who only indulged in pleasures of the flesh when he needed to settle his nerves. He never chose women from his pack, but instead would couple with unmated women in the territory. It wasn't often, but he had no other options since he didn't believe in self-gratification. It showed a lack of control, so it was a habit he'd given up over four hundred years ago.

Yet as his pants slipped to the floor and he looked at his erection in the mirror, carnal images of Kat tangled in his thoughts. He switched off the light and stripped down the covers, lying on silken sheets. At first it began with a touch, just a simple stroke to the head when he remembered the way Kat had pressed up against him earlier that evening. He'd known she wasn't wearing a bra beneath her shirt when her nipples hardened against his chest.

His promise to help her find Alex had filled him with a sense of purpose. A Packmaster's life was demanding, but he often missed the days when decisions were made by actions and not words. This beguiling woman had managed to make him feel more alive in one night than he had in centuries.

An image flashed in his mind of Kat's nude body straddling the back of the Mage and the way she swung her eyes up to Prince's with willful determination. He arched his back as he imagined what it would feel like to be the man beneath her—to have a Shifter as dominant as she astride him, her hips rocking, her sable eyes latched on his. An insatiable craving began.

One that made him relinquish a vow he'd made four hundred years ago.

CHAPTER 6

"**H**EY, HONEYPIE."

"Denver, what are you doing here?" Nadia said from a short distance away.

Kat groaned into her pillow and rubbed her face against it, squinting as she peered toward the front hallway to see what was going on.

"Look, I just wanted to stop by because I feel kind of shitty about how things went. It wasn't your fault; you were great. I've just found the girl I want and—"

Nadia's voice was smooth like honey. "No need to explain. If you want the truth, I think you can do better, but I don't believe in competing for any man's attention. My love life is not a game show."

The man named Denver chuckled and leaned against the doorjamb. "Did you ever watch *The Love Connection?*"

Kat smiled, since she loved game shows.

Denver was easy on the eyes, with blond hair and a cartoon character on his T-shirt. Although Kat was too far away to see what it said, she could have sworn it was *Fraggle Rock*. He seemed like the kind of guy Kat would normally hang out with, so naturally it came as a surprise that he and Nadia had been dating.

"Is that all you wanted to say?" Nadia asked, folding her arms.

"I've been thinking about what happened all week and… I don't want you to think I'm a dick. We just weren't peanut butter and jelly together. Anyhow, Naya respects you, and uh… I hope you don't hold this against her."

"So *that's* what this visit is about. Don't be ridiculous. Naya's a good friend who's connected me with a number of buyers. I'm not petty enough to punish her for a service I paid for." A moment of awkward silence fell between the two. Nadia inspected her shoes. "Are you sure you won't change your mind?"

Denver hiked up his baggy jeans—shredded at the knees—and plucked a piece of candy from his pocket. It looked like a gumball or jawbreaker and caused his left cheek to puff out when he attempted to smile. "That's one thing I'm sure of. This is a permanent deal and, no offense, but there's no way in Hades I could do any better. Anyhow, just wanted to smooth things over and make sure I didn't mess up your business relationship with Naya. I'll keep my eyes open, but I don't know what kind of men you go for."

"That won't be necessary. I'm not looking for a mate. Give your woman my best."

The blond-haired man inched into the hallway and waved before turning away.

Nadia slammed the door and Kat sat up, eyes alert.

Habit.

"I wasn't sure if you were going to sleep until noon or get up with the civilized world. Am I okay to leave you here alone today?" Nadia glanced at her slim gold watch, which complemented her olive-green pencil skirt and white blouse. Her hair was beautifully combed and parted down the middle.

Kat rubbed her eyes and blew her hair out of her face. Mornings were her least favorite time of day. "Given I don't have any pants, that kind of limits my daily agenda. I promise I won't paint anything, if that's what you're concerned about." She briefly looked at the floor and made sure her dagger was where she'd left it.

"I'm asking nicely for you to keep Prince out of our affairs. Promise me."

"I doubt I'll ever see him again after last night, but I'm not about to turn down help if he offers it. I have a strong lead on finding our father, and don't roll your eyes."

"It does no good to get your hopes up." Nadia lifted her purse from the chair in the hall. "I'm going to work. I have several artifacts to appraise for some important clients. No parties, no rearranging anything, no borrowing my clothes, no eating my ice cream, and no dragging any Packmasters on one of your crazy chases."

"Say *no* much?" Kat stood up and closed the distance between them, annoyed with all the orders being barked at her. She hadn't even had her morning sugar yet. "I won't even borrow your toothbrush, if that makes you happy. You'll barely know I'm here."

Satisfied, Nadia opened the door and paused. "Did you order something?"

"What is it?"

Curious, Kat shouldered past Nadia and peered into the outside hall. Someone had left a large paper bag in front of the door—not the kind you get grocery shopping, but the fancy kind with the arched handles. Kat bent down and reached inside, pulling out a pair of jeans, two blouses with spaghetti straps, a toothbrush, comb, and underwear—sexy black ones at that.

"What *is* all this?" Nadia peered down the empty hall in search of the person who'd left it.

Kat held Prince's business card between two fingers. When she turned it over, she saw that he'd signed *Charming* on the back. "Looks like they're from a knight in shining armor named Prince."

Nadia huffed and straightened her skirt. "Most men buy flowers for their date, not underwear for their date's *sister*."

"He's old school and probably thinks the way to impress you is by taking care of your family. If he didn't like you, he wouldn't be trying so hard to help your needy sister. Oh look, he even bought me a razor."

"Needy indeed. I have to go, Katarina. Call me if you need anything, and remember the rules!"

Nadia flew out in a rush, a heavy scent of perfume trailing behind her.

Kat yawned loudly and shuffled into the kitchen in search of something to eat.

"Dangit, Nads. Why didn't you put the pizza in there like I asked you to?" she grumbled, moving aside strange fruits and cheeses. If there was one thing her sister loved, it was gourmet cheese. And the weirder the animal it came from, the better. Kat couldn't even stand blue cheese on her salads; it made her gag. But whatever artificial goodness they sprinkled on pizza was all right with her.

Kat heaved a sigh and went to the bathroom to brush her teeth. She took her goodie bag with her, and once there, decided to hop in the shower. The stench of cigarettes still clung to her hair and was making her nauseous. Kat tossed her plaid shirt into the dryer with one of those scented sheets. The shirt had become a souvenir of a great night. Not the part where her suspect had gotten loose, but all the other stuff with Prince. Although keeping an item to remember time spent with her sister's boyfriend seemed a tad inappropriate.

While she soaked beneath the spray of hot water, Kat thought about the dream she'd had the previous night. It had seemed so vivid, walking into a dark room where Prince was lying naked on a bed. He called to her, and his wolf howled in the darkness before they made love.

Kat shivered just thinking about it. After she towel-dried her hair, she examined the jeans Prince had chosen for her. They were the kind that hung low on a woman's hips—comfy in all the right places.

"Snug!" Kat said approvingly, looking at her reflection in the mirror from all angles. What she loved was that he hadn't bought her fancy clothes in an attempt to make her into someone she wasn't.

She slipped into a white tank top that didn't quite cover up her cleavage the way she would have liked. It seemed peculiar he would have bought her such a tight shirt, the kind that left nothing to the imagination if the temperature dropped. Luckily the plaid shirt was nice and warm after a tumble in the dryer, so she rolled up the sleeves to her elbows and grabbed her sneakers, wishing he had left her some good running shoes instead of all the clothes.

After tying her sneakers, she dashed to the fridge one last time. Kat twisted open a large jar of pickles and stuffed a big dill into her mouth.

"Time to head out," she mumbled, grabbing her car keys.

The second Kat opened the door, she stumbled over a shoelace that had come undone. Prince caught her arms just as she was falling to her knees. She lifted her eyes up to his and, oh God, *the visual*. There she was, kneeling before a Packmaster with a pickle wedged so deep in her mouth that she started to gag.

Kat slowly pulled it out, and it made a juicy sound when she sucked on the tip. "I almost choked on that thing."

His lip twitched, and wow, did he look yummy. Kat admired his fitted black shirt and dark jeans.

She wobbled as she stood up, doing a quick check to make sure his fly wasn't open. "Are you wearing denims? I'm thoroughly impressed at your attempt to blend in with the natives."

He folded his arms and assessed her attire. "Are the garments I provided to your satisfaction?"

"You talk like a commercial," she said, biting off a chunk of the pickle and locking the door behind her. "They're great. Thanks. I'm not even going to ask how you know my exact size."

"I'm a perceptive man."

"That I don't doubt. You bought me lace panties. No one's ever bought me sexy panties before." Kat took another bite from her pickle and suddenly felt self-conscious about the way he kept staring at her mouth. "So, do you want to start brainstorming on where we should look first? My contact gave me the names of two bars. They're not his regular hangouts, but the bartender or some of the waitresses might have information."

Kat lost her train of thought, disappointed that Prince had tied his hair back again. She spied a short silver hair on the side of his head and quickly looked away.

"I scheduled a meeting to sell you at noon."

Kat almost choked on her pickle for real. "Whoa," she blurted out, holding up her hands. "I don't know what you think we have going on here, but I'm not a two-bedroom condo. You can't just sell me."

They turned around and walked a few paces toward the elevator. Prince smelled so good that Kat kept falling behind so she could catch his heavenly draft.

He pushed the elevator button and folded his arms. "Vlad is in the slave trade, as you're aware. With what little we know, my associate suggested that Vlad's probably a middleman."

"Yeah, that's my thought too. Buys them from his contacts and turns around to sell them for a higher price, taking all the risk.

Sellers usually want to flip them over as fast as they can so they don't get busted, and sometimes it's not easy to find a buyer that quickly." She gave him a skeptical look. "Do you really think this plan will work? With the higher authority hiring more bounty hunters, a lot of the sellers are skittish about dealing with people they don't know."

"I have access to a list of traders across the continent who've made transactions within the past ten years. There aren't as many big ones as you might think, so with the help of an associate, I was able to narrow it down to the two men we had the least information on who might be Vlad. The others were easily ruled out. An insider took a big risk and referred me to them. Our first appointment is at noon, the second at three."

She pressed the elevator button five times and leaned on the door, rolling the pickle between her thumb and index finger. "Why did you space them so far apart?"

Prince relaxed his stance, letting his arms fall to his sides. Kat tried not to notice the ropes of taut muscle along his arms. It was a travesty how he kept such a stunning physique hidden beneath his suits, so seeing him in a T-shirt was like going to a carnival and finding out no one was standing in line for your favorite ride.

"I thought we could have lunch."

"Sounds amazing. First we'll sell my body and then we'll grab some tacos."

The elevator doors opened and Kat slipped through the opening, catching herself before slamming against the rear wall. She casually raked her fingers through her hair and yawned before nibbling on her breakfast. Prince eyed her as he got in, looking at her the way most people did—like he didn't know what to think of her odd behavior.

When he knelt down in front of her, she sucked in a sharp breath.

Prince began lacing up her sneakers, tying them with double knots so they wouldn't come undone. "You should try the running shoes with the sticky straps."

"You mean Velcro?" The mere thought of her chasing down an outlaw in Velcro shoes was enough to give her the giggles. Kat unabashedly cradled his head with one hand, running her fingers over his smooth hair. "You should wear your hair loose."

"It gets in the way," he said, tightening her other shoe.

"Then why bother growing it? Shave it all off if you don't care."

He peered up at her with his blue eye, which was his left one. It was a striking shade, like a sapphire stone sparkling beneath moonlight. The other was an ordinary shade of melted chocolate, but together they were fascinating.

The elevator doors opened, and Nadia's neighbor stood at the entrance with her little white dog in her arms. Her eyes widened at Prince on his knees and Kat holding his head.

"He's almost finished," Kat said in a breathy voice.

Prince snapped his head back to look and then quickly stood up. The woman's eyes were glued to him, and he bowed slightly, holding the elevator door open for Kat while giving her a punishing glance.

She sauntered out and petted the little dog on the head as they passed. The old woman unabashedly gawked at them, and it amused Kat how easily humans were offended by such trivial innuendoes.

Her back straightened like an arrow when Prince placed his hand against the curve of her spine.

"You're mischievous, Kat."

"Don't try to pretend that wasn't funny," she said, pointing back at the elevators. "There's nothing better in life than someone getting the wrong idea. Didn't you ever watch *Three's Company*? Oh wait, you don't watch television. See what you're missing?"

He veered her toward the right. "I'll drive."

Kat took one look at his Audi and chortled. Prince was definitely not a low-end-model kind of guy. "Yeah, we're not going to stand out *at all*. So where are we going to meet contestant number one?"

"His apartment."

She stopped in front of his car and looked up at him, the sun shining in her eyes. "I don't know if that's such a good idea. Coffee shops and bars are always safer bets, especially with guys who are into flesh trading. What if he has a myriad of helpers in there ready to pounce and put me up for sale?"

Prince rested his hands on her shoulders, giving her a pensive stare. "Then I'll protect you."

His words penetrated down to her feet, giving her the kind of reassurance and feeling of being protected that only an alpha could.

Kat bit into the end of her pickle, the crunch tearing through the awkward silence. "Like last night? You almost crushed me to death. Although watching you flip over that table was a little gallant and raised a few hairs on my arms. Do you carry a weapon?"

"*I* am the weapon."

Kat sucked on the tip of the pickle and then smiled. "Good answer, Charming. Are you going to open the car door for me like a gentleman, or would you rather watch me slide over the hood and climb in through the window? Either way, I'm good."

He spun on his heel and rounded the car. Kat followed close behind, her grin widening. Not many men looked as good going as they did coming, but Prince had a masculine swagger she couldn't ignore. She wondered if he was kidding about being the weapon, but men his age didn't crack jokes very often. Either way, remarks like that made her want to figure him out.

Prince gingerly lifted the handle of the door, and she tossed the remainder of her pickle on the curb and got in.

"No one should be that good-looking," she mused quietly, watching him walk around the front of the car. His seemingly innocuous gaze made her warm all over, and his eyes were predatory, humbling her with centuries of experience. That man was like a walking powder keg.

When Prince got in and shut the door, he gave her a cursory glance. "Why didn't you toss out that garment?"

"This?" she asked, tugging on the flannel threads. "I kind of like it. It keeps everything concealed better, and I don't just mean my breasts."

"Are you armed?"

She reclined the seat back a few inches and stretched her legs. "I *am* the weapon," she replied with a playful smirk. "What's good to eat around this town?"

He started the car and merged into traffic. "I know a few restaurants that will find us a space quickly."

Kat pulled down her visor to shield her eyes from the blinding sun reflecting off a mirrored building. "No, thanks. I like grab-and-go food. So… how many Breeds live in Austin? I've never really gone out and immersed myself in the local culture. Nadia says she loves it here because of the eclectic atmosphere, but it's all new to me."

"We have more Shifters than most cities," he began. "Here you have the best of both worlds: plenty of land for packs to purchase and close to a big city. Many young humans are drawn to the live music, barbecue, and nightlife; it's a place where differences are celebrated. Naturally, we blend in."

She flipped one of the shoelaces around where she'd crossed her foot over her knee. "Swell. My kind of town. Packs or rogues?"

He pulled a pair of mirrored sunglasses out and slipped them on. "An abundance of each. Enough to keep the Council busy."

Kat squinted from the bright sun. The used-car lots and Mexican restaurants alongside the road drew her attention away, as did the man on the unicycle. Every so often they'd pass a homeless man lying in the grass, or someone holding up a sign advertising gold exchange.

"Do you consort with other Breeds much?" Prince asked.

Kat wondered about that statement. What he *really* wanted to know was what kind of men were in her dating pool. Mating outside your Breed was frowned upon, although most dated other Breeds once or twice out of curiosity. To be honest, Kat didn't have an interest in dating men who weren't Shifters. Most Chitahs didn't like her dangerous profession and were always trying to defend her honor. Sweet, but a little embarrassing for a bounty hunter. Vampires were another story. They had the ability to charm people into doing things with a form of hypnotism, so Kat didn't trust Vamps as far as she could throw them. She'd dated a Mage once, and he was a decent guy, but the sex was too weird since he couldn't touch her. They'd get charged up with energy during sex, making their hands deadly weapons—except with another Mage. Kat really didn't want to explore the world of electrocution by sex, so she took them off the menu.

It's not that her lovers had been bad, but few met her needs and most of the time she could have placed bets on when the sex was going to happen. Kat lived a spontaneous life, so planned sex had zero appeal. And it's not like they had an itinerary, but after splurging on an expensive dinner and telling her about nine hundred times how sexy she was, intercourse was always an expectation.

Not that Kat had much sex.

Maybe that's why she kept gawking at Prince like a woman whose ovaries had just come out of hibernation and were about to implode. Her stupid wolf had a thing for alpha males, and she had scented him right from the start. Her inner tail was wagging, so Kat needed to pull it together before she mounted him at the next red light. The one thing that steered her alpha hormones in the other direction was knowing that Prince was one of those planners who strategically placed rose petals on the floor, creating a trail to his private chambers.

A trail Nadia would soon follow.

"Well?" he pressed.

She'd forgotten the question.

"I was asking if you associate with other Breeds," he reminded her.

She scratched her cheek and watched a little boy in the car in front of them stick out his tongue. "It depends."

"On?"

"If they're dickheads. I'm not sure what exactly you want to know, since you're pretty good about beating around the bush."

"I dislike that idiom."

She snapped her gaze at him. "Well, I dislike euphemisms. *Associate with other Breeds?* Why don't you say what you really mean? Not that it's any of your business, but yes, I've dated non-Shifters."

"You're an alpha wolf," he ground out. "Your standards should be higher. You could have your selection of any Packmaster you desired."

She snorted and stretched her legs. "Yeah, they're just beating down my door to put their claim on a bounty hunter who sometimes forgets to shave and likes to watch TV all day. I'm a real collector's item."

"These are traits you can change."

"My tummy's all aflutter at your compliment. Look, I'm not changing who I am," she bit out, sitting up straight in her seat. "Oh, wow. There's a taco stand! Let's hit that on the way back." Kat twisted around in her seat and stared through the back windshield at the little shack on the left side of the road. "And they sell quesadillas. Put that intersection to memory."

Kat faced forward, and the silence that followed turned into an awkward moment. "What?"

He looked sideways at her with his brown eye. "You're unpredictable. I never know what you'll say or do next."

"Thanks," she replied sincerely. Kat didn't dwell on hidden meanings.

"Are you upset with me?"

She felt bad for a minute because he was serious. Kat sometimes had an abrasive personality, but she didn't like to hold grudges. "We had a disagreement. That's all."

He pulled the car up to an urban apartment building—the kind with indoor elevators and no balconies. When Kat got out, she could feel the heat rising from the concrete, telling her it was going to be a scorcher.

A few tufts of cottonwood floated in the air, and she rubbed her nose. "What do we do if it's not Vlad?"

"We decline his offer for lemonade?"

She patted his arm, holding his bicep long enough to sigh inwardly at how strong he felt. "You're funny, Charming. I *knew* there was a sense of humor hiding in there. Stick with me long enough and you might crack a smile."

When they reached the main door to the building, Prince paused and traced a finger over his eyebrow. Kat watched his reflection in the glass, wondering why he was hesitant about going in. Probably having second thoughts.

"I don't think this is him," she said, adjusting her white tank top and then rolling up her sleeves.

"What makes you say that?" he asked as they moved through the doors.

Her voice reverberated off the beige walls of the first floor. "I know a few things about Vlad that aren't in the records—unsavory things you don't want to know about." She smoothed her hand along the walls, studying how close together the apartments were. "These are tight living quarters. Too many people can hear what he's up to. I can't believe they don't even lock the main doors. *Anyone* could walk in."

"This is it," he said quietly.

Kat glanced down the hall to make sure they had privacy. "Go ahead and knock; I'll hang back."

Prince cleared his throat and rapped his knuckles against the door. Kat went into ready mode, her heart ticking fast as she prepared for anything. Footsteps reached the other side of the door and then fell silent as he was probably looking through the peephole. She stepped out of sight and left Prince standing with his back to the door so Vlad wouldn't recognize him.

The door opened a crack. "Yeah?" a husky voice said.

In a motion too fast to track, Prince shoved the door open.

Kat rushed inside and looked at a short man in blue pajama bottoms who was backing away from them. The apartment smelled like brownies, and her mouth instantly watered.

"What's this about?" the bald man asked in a shaky voice.

Kat glanced at the window behind him in the living room and realized why he'd chosen to live on the first floor. A large man emerged from the shadows and approached them, one who was twice her size. His eyes were thin slivers and he looked like a man who had spent time in a boxing ring. Not just because of his build, but his nose was crooked and face misshapen. As he moved into the light, her eyes drifted down to the ominous tattoo across his chest of a warrior holding a battle-axe above his head, blood on the tip of the blade, and riding a black horse with eyes like the devil.

Prince shoved the smaller man against the wall. "I have it on good authority that you're selling young girls. Consider this your warning. I'm one of the most powerful Packmasters in this territory, and the torturous things I could inflict on your body would frighten your ancestors. Heed my warning, coward. If you so much as jaywalk across the street, I'm coming for you."

"Yeah?" he countered in a wavering voice. "Tell that to my friend."

"Not a bad idea," Kat suggested, watching Mr. Scary Tattoo with bated breath.

Prince wrenched open a closet door and shoved the pajama man in, then dragged a heavy table in front of the closed door.

"I got it," Kat said with cool confidence, strutting toward the tatted man. She was reaching for her dagger when Prince caught her arm.

"Let me handle this."

She peered over her shoulder. "I'll subdue him while you make besties with the little guy."

A look of irritation flashed in his eyes. "I'll not have you fight this man in my stead."

Kat's jaw set and she stepped back, her brows arched. "Fine. When you're done crippling peabrain over there, the damsel in distress will be in the kitchen."

She turned away, struggling to conceal her smile. It should have insulted her, but truthfully, Kat was kind of awestruck with his chivalry. Plus, she really wanted to see how he handled himself, and if she was lucky enough, maybe she'd get a look at his wolf.

While Prince laid down his threats, Kat wandered into the kitchen and watched them through the wide entryway. The other man didn't say a word, and she couldn't tell his Breed but assumed he was probably a Shifter. Based on the fact he hadn't shifted yet, odds were he wasn't a dangerous animal. Most likely he was just a rabbit or deer. Usually the docile animals were the ones who went overboard on their tough-guy image so people wouldn't mess with them, afraid that they might be a grizzly.

The two men exploded into action. Kat held her breath, enthralled by Prince's raw abilities. The man could fight, and not just modern moves with punching and roundhouse kicks. His actions were fast and precise. A picture flew off the wall and the glass frame broke into two pieces. When they moved out of sight, she peered into the hall. A chair flew in her direction, and she backed away as it crashed against the front door.

Kat strolled back into the kitchen and studied the contents of the fridge while chaos erupted in the living room. "Doesn't anyone keep leftover Chinese anymore?" She cracked open a can of ginger ale and took a sip while bodies slammed against the walls in the other room. When it got quiet, she cocked her head and listened for movement.

"Charming?" she called out.

A maniacal laugh sounded from the little weasel locked in the closet.

Kat set the can on the counter and hurried toward the hallway, just in time to see Prince barefoot in jeans, pulling his T-shirt over his head.

"Dammit," she whispered to herself, having missed his shift.

Disappointment flared when she saw he'd already pulled his hair back. She glanced at the body but couldn't see the gory aftermath in the dark room. It didn't take a genius to figure out Prince had either ripped out the man's throat or somehow asphyxiated him. Kat was thoroughly impressed with how fast Prince had taken down such an impressive fighter. She thought they would have been at it for at least five minutes.

While he put on his shoes, she returned to the kitchen and nabbed a brownie from an oversized plate on the stove. It even had the powdered sugar on top she loved so much.

"Leave town and find another profession," Prince shouted at the closet door as he left the apartment.

Kat followed behind him, and her lips eased into a grin. "You're pretty good at this. Sure you don't want to be a bounty hunter? I could always use a partner. We could be Mulder and Scully. Cagney and Lacey. Scooby-Doo and—"

He snatched the brownie from her hand and tossed it into a tall trash can.

"Hey! I was going to eat that," she protested.

Kat was sucking the powder off her finger when he suddenly grabbed her wrists and wrenched them away. She watched in astonishment as he used her plaid shirt to wipe her fingers clean.

"I'm amazed anyone would want to do this for a living, let alone a beautiful woman. And that brownie you just put in your mouth was probably laced with narcotics to sedate his next victim. He's selling Shifters into slavery; do you think they go willingly?"

He wiped at her mouth, and a tiny bit of terror raced through her as she spat on the floor. Kat should have known better, but her appetite had gotten the best of her, along with having Prince as a distraction.

"If you start to feel dizzy, I'm taking you back to Nadia's," he stated.

She knocked his hand away and stormed off. "I'm fine. I barely licked off enough of that sugar to have done any serious damage. Now let's eat some tacos and get this day over with." Kat pushed the main door open, her faced heated with embarrassment and anger all at once. "By the way, you're a terrible partner!"

<hr />

"These are sooo yummy," Kat sang, rocking back and forth in her metal chair, biting into her taco. "Spicy, *spiiicy*."

Prince eyed her impatiently while finishing the last of his beef burrito. By the time they'd stopped off at the taco stand, the effects of whatever drug Kat had consumed from the brownie topping were beginning to show. She wasn't sleepy or knocked out, but her altered behavior was similar to someone who was inebriated or stoned.

He decided that when she finished her sixth taco they were leaving. She had already been eyeing the beef nachos, and this buffet had to end or they'd never make it to the second location.

"Do you have any brothers or sisters?" she asked, wiggling her fingers in front of her face.

"I had a brother once, but he perished long ago in a great battle."

"Sorry. That must have been hard for you."

Prince appreciated Kat's sincerity, and her honesty was refreshing.

"It must be lonely not to have any family left." Kat sucked on her straw, and it made a terrible slurping sound when the soda reached the bottom. She gave it a shake and the ice rattled. "I don't know what I'd do without my sister."

"What about your mother?"

"She left us for good." Kat set down the yellow cup and a gust of wind blew some of her dark hair forward, but she didn't make any attempt to fix it. "I checked up on her a few years ago, but she's hard to track since she's still with that rogue and they move around a lot. I think her pregnancy was an accident, and maybe two babies at once was too much for her to handle. I guess I'm used to her being gone since I'd only lived with her a few years of my life. But my papa is my heart, and so is Nadia. Maybe she's Tweedledee and I'm Tweedledum, but we're two tweedles, you know?"

The effects of the drug were beginning to wear off, although not entirely. He much preferred when she was talkative and happy to this altered version of herself that was sullen and introspective.

"My pack is my family." Prince wadded up the empty burrito wrapper.

"Are they? Do you hang out with them and watch TV?"

"You have a fixation on television."

She shrugged and sat back. "Everyone has their thing. Nadia loves nice clothes and those breakable figurines, my papa loves fishing, and I love reruns of *Seinfeld*."

"As I recall, your father was a skilled hunter."

She flashed a dazzling smile and looked up at the sky. "He is. More with a crossbow than a gun, but he really loves fishing. Sometimes we'd take a camping trip and spend all day on the lake in a small boat. He's like a fish whisperer or something—you should have *seen* the ones he caught. Afterward, we'd cook them up and then he'd tell stories over a campfire. He tells great stories."

Prince couldn't help but notice how she spoke of her father in the present tense. Kat truly believed with her whole heart that Alex was still alive. "Yes, he did. Your father weaved some tall tales."

She laughed and wadded up her wrapper, setting it next to the other five. "That's the truth. Half the time I wasn't sure if he was making it up."

Prince drew a deep breath, taking in the smells and sounds of the street corner around them. Taco meat, hot concrete, summer wind, honeysuckle growing over the concrete wall behind them. "Every story your father told had some truth to it; he just happened to be a master at embellishing the boring parts."

Kat leaned back in her chair. "How did you meet?"

"I'd wandered into his territory and fell on a steel trap. My injuries were severe, and I could have lost my leg. When he discovered me, I thought he was going to take my head for trespassing. I was an alpha, and we both knew I had intentionally ignored the territorial markings. In those days, that blatant disregard was an act of war. A Packmaster had the right to slay any alpha who crossed into his domain."

"Why didn't he?"

"Because Alex liked to see the good in men. He had foresight most men didn't and chose to release me from the trap and take me in. I was looking for a fresh start, and he gave me men from his own pack. He wanted us to be allies, but we became brothers by circumstance."

Prince could see a glimmer of Alex in Kat's eyes, and he felt a pang of remorse for the absence of his friend.

Kat tipped her head to the side, averting her gaze. "What were the women like in those times?"

Prince thought back, uncertain of how to answer since he had lived in many different centuries. A woman's role varied by country, time period, and Breed. Shifter women had always had some level of power. "In Russia, women were warriors. I met two who were second-in-commands. Italian women preferred to have the men go to battle, so there's never been one rule."

"What were you fighting over?"

He rubbed his jaw, deep in thought. "Land. Councils enforce rules and distribute land, but before they came into existence, packs were vulnerable to greedy alphas. Land meant power, and

Packmasters weren't just assembling a family; we were building an army to protect what was ours."

She sighed wistfully and rested her chin in the palm of her hand. "I could listen to you talk for hours."

He dwelled on her comment for a moment. "Tell me, why do you prefer television over real people?"

Kat studied one of her short fingernails. "Because I can turn it off when I'm sick of it. Most of the people I meet are on the job. I haven't really met anyone I connect with—someone I can talk to about anything who's actually interested in what I have to say. I guess watching TV gives me a spoonful of that life I'm missing out on. I can't afford to make friends in this line of work; I'm always on the move."

"Have you considered working as a private investigator? I know a man who might be able to help, and it's local work doing essentially the same thing."

A gust of wind lifted her hair, and she tucked it behind her ear. "I'd need a reason to stay. Nadia's my sister, but she's got her own life, and I'm not a huge part of it. She's not reason enough to throw my anchor off the ship. I like the idea of working as a PI, but it's the kind of job that keeps you rooted in one place. I'm not sure where home is."

Prince wanted to say more, but instead he stood up and tossed their wrappers into the trash. "We should go before it gets too late. Are you feeling well enough to do this today?"

Her eyes widened comically as she tried to rouse herself from a drug-induced state of mind. "My wolf is fed, I've got twenty-four ounces of sugar coursing through my veins… Yep. I should be fine."

She turned, and Prince realized he was standing on her shoelace. Before she took a step, he wrapped his arms around her and pulled her against him. She fit in his arms perfectly, and his blood heated when she reached up and held on to his neck. Kat had lovely eyes, the kind of shifting color he could stare at for hours. They seemed to change color, and right now the sunlight had transformed them into the most indescribable shade of gold.

Her voice relaxed to a sultry sound that a man might hear in bed. "Nadia's a lucky woman."

"I'm going to kiss you," he said, inviting no argument.

She said nothing, but her lips parted as if daring him to try. He licked his own, and when her gaze settled on his mouth, it sent a spike of need through him that awakened his wolf. A desire so intense that he pulled her in tighter to feel more of her soft body against his.

Prince leaned down and pressed a chaste kiss to her lips. He moaned softly when he realized she tasted like honey, a sweet elixir on his tongue that made him grow hard with need. When he intensified the kiss, she grew limp in his arms and he drew back.

Kat's eyes were closed—she'd passed out.

CHAPTER 7

⟶⟵

"**W**AKE UP, KAT."

A sharp voice cut through the darkness and pulled her awake. She was in the passenger seat of Prince's Audi, seat reclined, parked in the woods, oak trees shading the windshield.

Disoriented from the time lapse, Kat took a deep breath and sat up straight. "Where are we?"

"I didn't want to wake you since you were still under the influence of drugs. But it's almost three in the afternoon, and we're losing time. We need to find out if this is Vlad."

"Give me a second to wake up. My leg's asleep." Kat lifted her right leg and put her foot on the dash. Her muscles were stiff, not exactly the condition she wanted to be in when going on a chase. She massaged her calf and yawned. "So suspect number two lives out here in the deep, dark woods? I don't like this, Charming. Not one bit. There's nowhere to corner him."

"You said you followed him to Austin? If this is Vlad, then perhaps this is just a rental and he's ill-prepared for an ambush."

She put her foot down and studied their surroundings. "Uh-huh. But his plates are Texas, so I'm willing to bet this is home sweet home. If that's the case, he probably has steel traps in the woods or a bunch of goons protecting his property. Why don't we hang out by the main road and just tail him when he leaves? Slow and steady wins the race."

Prince unbuckled his seat belt. "And where is the fun in that?"

She blinked as he got out of the car. "Great. I'm on a mission with John McClane."

"Who?"

Oops. Kat hadn't meant for him to hear that. Too many nights watching *Die Hard*.

"Never mind," she said, quietly shutting her door. "Where's the house?"

He pointed up the dirt road. "Just around the curve."

"He won't get far without his car." Kat rolled her eyes while adjusting the strap that wrapped around her midsection, making sure her shirt concealed it. "God, I hate it when I rhyme. Anyhow, we should slash his tires before knocking to make sure he doesn't try to escape. Although, he *is* a Mage and might flash to town."

"Doubtful," Prince said quietly, walking on her left. "Vlad doesn't run; he attacks."

She tried to keep her voice low, but walking made her breathe harder. "By the way, if something happens and I shift, stay away from my dagger. Obviously my wolf can't use it, but she'll take off your hand if you try to disarm her."

"Duly noted."

"Just so you know, I really don't want to let my wolf out. She's never met your wolf, and that could get ugly. So I'm going to do what I can to keep her in check."

The property wasn't paved, nor had anyone laid down gravel. Kat walked quietly on the dirt, thinking what a mess it must be when it rained. When they rounded the corner, she paused behind an overgrown bush. The one-story home worked to their advantage since it offered fewer places for someone to hide, although she would have preferred wood to brick since it was easier to set on fire. One car meant he was probably alone, and there weren't any animals to announce their presence. The blinds were closed—every one of them. Either this guy had something to hide or he was allergic to sunlight.

Kat gripped Prince's bicep. "Hey, just in case I shift, do me a favor and stay in human form."

"Why would I do that if it means putting you in danger?"

"Because you're an alpha and you'll be able to get me to shift back. Sometimes my wolf is a stubborn partner and doesn't want to give up control."

Humor danced in his eyes. "I'm familiar with that feeling."

Kat poked him in the ribs. "Very funny. If he takes off in his car, my wolf will try to chase him down on the freeway. She did it once," Kat said, strolling toward the house. "I ended up with blistered hands and feet and had to shift a couple of times to heal. I'm not going through *that* again. Shall we knock?"

Her attention drifted down to the cigarette butts littering the cement porch. She remembered Vlad smoking in the bar where she'd first seen him. Kat wrinkled her nose and held her knuckles against the door, frozen in thought. If they knocked, would Vlad be stupid enough to just open up? As much as she loved feebleminded criminals, she had a feeling that wouldn't be the case with him.

Her mind began dissecting their situation. This wasn't going to work. He was expecting an exchange. The last thing she needed for him to barricade himself in the house with weapons.

Kat tied her flannel shirt around her waist and got on her knees, her long hair shielding her face.

"What are you doing?" Prince hissed.

"Take your hair out of the ponytail."

"What?"

She peered up at him, her voice at a whisper. "He's going to recognize you. Ponytails aren't exactly the popular trend. Scramble up your hair a little and let's play this out. He's probably going to peek through the window so he can get a better look at who he's dealing with." She gestured toward the glass. "He's only ever seen you in a suit, so let's not tip him off. We just need him to open the door."

"And then?" Prince removed the elastic band, shaking his hair loose.

Kat forgot her name. As soon as his lush, dark hair came unbound, it slipped in front of his face and gave her goose bumps. He didn't look like a prince anymore; he looked like a king. She swallowed thickly and leaned against his leg, wanting to rub all over him like a cat in heat.

"Hold me by my hair," she said.

Prince reached down and gently grabbed a handful of her hair, sending tiny prickles across her spine. When he knocked on the door several times, her heart leapt into her throat. This was going to look really stupid if it didn't turn out to be Vlad.

After a moment, the door hinges creaked. "James?"

"Yep," Prince replied.

Kat smiled, remembering when she'd asked rhetorically if he ever just answered with a *yep*.

"You must be new to this line of work. Usually they come drugged and bound. You'll find out when one of them gets away and you're out money."

Kat instantly recognized the voice as Vlad's.

"I beat her into submission," Prince said. "Step outside and I'll show you the goods."

Kat watched patiently as he drew closer.

"Wait a second... I remember those shoes." Vlad stopped in his tracks and backed up a step.

She flipped her hair back and bounced to her feet. "You better believe it, Dracula, because they're going to be kicking your ass in about two seconds!"

Vlad narrowed his eyes at Prince and splayed his fingers, sharpening his Mage light.

Kat's stunner was infused with enough magic to paralyze him— if she could just get him to stand still long enough for her to drive it into his chest.

As if their minds were linked, Prince and Kat began to space apart and flank Vlad from either side.

Vlad reached out to grab her wrist, and she snapped it back, tightening her grip on the knife. Prince rushed Vlad and managed to get his right arm locked behind his back, but Vlad struck him in the face with his elbow and maneuvered out of his grip. They fought with incredible speed and agility—Prince holding his own in hand-to-hand combat against a Mage.

"You're moving too fast!" Kat yelled, flustered at the thought that she might end up stabbing Prince in the neck instead of Vlad. It wasn't easy to get her hands on a good stunner, and Kat didn't want to chance losing her knife.

"Get back!" Prince said in clipped words.

"Did you really just say that to a bounty hunter?" she asked, twirling the knife in her hand. "I'm going to stab you if you don't get out of the way."

Prince slammed Vlad against the wall, hand on his throat. "You scum. I've waited centuries to get my hands on you."

Vlad put his hands up as if he were going to gouge out Prince's eyes. "You left Russia like a dog with its tail between its legs."

Prince roared and flew back two feet, covering his eyes.

It took Kat a minute before she realized he'd taken a blast of energy to the face. She sprang forward and lunged with the dagger, but Vlad flashed around her.

"Fight like a man!" she yelled, turning around.

"Only if you fight like a woman." He glanced down at her jeans. "Are you sure you don't have a penis in there?"

"Are you goading me? Bad idea."

Prince lunged a nanosecond later, knocking Vlad off the porch and into the dirt. He struck him with repeated blows, but Vlad used his hands to shock Prince with more of his energy. Vlad struggled to his feet and gave his car a passing glance.

"Forget your keys?" Kat sang. "Come inside and get them. You're not going to get far without a car." Kat tapped the dagger against her thigh, irritated by her unintentional rhyme that made her sound like Dr. Seuss. "You can only flash for so long before I'll find you asleep in a ditch, drained like a dead battery. I'm willing to bet this Audi can drive a hell of a lot faster than you can sprint down the main freeway. All I want are answers. *Where* is my father?"

Vlad flashed forward and punched her in the face, leaving her no time to react. When he reached for the knife, she thrust it into his left side, but he moved too fast and it only pierced his flesh.

Kat's lip throbbed and she reacted in anger, slicing the blade in crisscross motions. With each swing, Vlad stepped farther out of reach.

A blood-curdling growl sounded to her right, sending a chill up her spine. From the corner of her eye, she could see Prince had shifted into a stunning black-and-grey wolf. The closer he stalked toward the house, the more she recognized him by his brown and blue eyes, a piercing contrast against his dark pelt.

Vlad backed up against the banister, cornered and eyeing the wolf.

"I'll leave you alone if you just give me what I want," she offered.

"Daddy's precious little girl can't let go, can she?" He settled his eyes on her in a different way this time. "Just how close were you two?"

"What the hell does *that* mean?"

Prince's wolf snarled, his fangs intimidating Vlad, who knew exactly how fast a wolf could strip flesh from bone.

"Did he leave you any parting gifts?"

Kat frowned and couldn't figure out his angle. Why did guys like him have to be so damn difficult? She thought he might be going for the incest jokes since that was the most common insult made toward wolf packs, but before she could formulate a reply, he flashed past her so heart-stoppingly fast that the force knocked her down. Stunned, Kat looked up just in time to see him leaping through the treetops.

"A Jumper. You slick little bastard, I should have known."

Prince's wolf took off after him like a torpedo, and Kat was left alone on the dirty porch with a trail of fire ants chilling out near her face, oblivious to the battle of giants happening all around them. Kat hopped up and put her dagger back in the sheath before going inside. Vlad wouldn't stay away for long, so this was a good opportunity to search his house.

"What was I thinking eating six tacos?" She groaned, rubbing her belly. Spicy food and hand-to-hand combat rarely mixed.

She did a quick check inside to make sure the house was empty, wishing she had brought her gun. "You live like a pig."

A beer can clacked against the dingy wall when she kicked it out of the way and sat on the living room sofa—a checkered monstrosity that was crying out for someone to take a blowtorch to it and put it out of its misery. She shuddered at the crusty stain on the carpet and reached for his laptop. The computer screen came up without a password lock.

"Not only that, but you're a tool. Didn't anyone ever teach you about password protection?"

Kat scrolled through his files. He'd labeled his folders in Russian, so she was able to figure out which ones were important. One had pictures of the Shifters he'd bought and sold, while another listed every transaction he'd made over the past ten years. Since he was an outlaw, he couldn't use a Breed bank without getting caught, even with an alias. Vlad must be hiding his money somewhere.

When the door creaked, she glanced over her shoulder at Prince and then turned away. He moved silently around the couch and knelt before her, his slender fingers lightly touching her face.

"Are you injured?"

"I almost had him, but he wiggled out of reach. Did your wolf tire out?"

Prince stood up and crossed the room behind her, rattling something in the quaint kitchen.

"Where do you think he keeps his money?" she yelled out. "Maybe we can hold it for ransom." The thought amused her and she laughed quietly.

Prince reappeared and pressed something cold to her face. She hissed and recoiled, trying to shove his arm away.

"Keep still. Your lip is bleeding. Do you want to shift to heal?"

"A little boo-boo on my face isn't traumatic enough to unleash my wolf. If it swells up to the size of a grapefruit, I'll do a quick shift, but right now I need to look through these files."

Kat took the ice-filled towel from him and held it against her mouth. Having a man fuss over her was bad enough, but the fact that she liked it wasn't helping matters.

"Can you search the house while I finish this up? Maybe we can find something of value and strike a bargain. I'd take the laptop, but I'm betting he has a backup and I'd rather him not know I've downloaded his files. Thoughts?"

Prince paced in front of her barefoot, and Kat couldn't tear her eyes away. His shoes must have still been in the yard, not that she had any complaints. Kat liked seeing a sexy man barefoot, just so long as he didn't have excessively hairy toes or something growing on them. Prince had nice feet—the kind that were probably bathed in scented oils and massaged by virgins.

When he moved out of sight, she reached beneath her shirt and pulled out a flash drive.

"What else do you have in there?" he asked with amusement, threading his long hair away from his face.

She plugged it in the side of the laptop and began copying files. "Having a good strap to hold my knife is great, but it also came with a few small pouches. I have a pack of gum in one, but I always carry a flash drive for opportunities like this." She pulled out a stick of cinnamon gum. "Want some?"

Kat expected him to berate her for foolishly fighting a Mage and then acting as if nothing had happened. That was how most people reacted to her job, and she could hardly blame him since she lived outside the lines of normalcy.

But Prince accepted the gum, folded it into his mouth, and sat on the couch beside her. That fluffed up her ego just a little bit, although Prince was a man who chose his words wisely and was probably taking his time to think of the right manner in which to reprimand her as all Packmasters loved to do.

"You have admirable control over your wolf," he said, bumping shoulders with her.

Kat ballooned with pride, attempting to suppress her smile. "We're a team. She knows when to hang tight and when to attack. This guy's gonna be hard to catch," she said, pulling out the flash drive.

"Next time give me the knife while you lock him in restraints."

Next time? she thought. It roused all kinds of emotions—a sense of camaraderie with someone who was willing to be her partner, even if it was just temporary. Someone who wanted to see this thing through until the end. Someone whose skin was brushing against her arm and giving her all kinds of indecent thoughts.

Mated wolves were amorous after battle. Prince wasn't her mate by a mile, but after seeing him in action today, she was having lustful thoughts about him fighting to protect her life. Her wolf was pacing anxiously within, signaling she was eager to be mounted.

"Oh, hell no," Kat blurted out. She snapped the laptop shut and sprang to her feet.

"Is something wrong?"

She dropped the bag of ice on his crotch and he tensed. "You sitting on that sofa, rubbing up against me, is what's wrong. You can't just sit there smelling good and speaking in that smoky voice like it's no big deal. And stop smiling with your eyes. They're sexy enough without you having to draw more attention to them. And don't compliment my wolf after battle; you *know* what effect that has on a Shifter. And put your hair back into that ponytail while you're at it. I can't concentrate with you walking around looking like a man who wears tear-away pants."

"Tear-away what?"

"You heard me, Charming. Search the house so we can get out of here. And next time you take me out for tacos, *three* is the legal limit."

CHAPTER 8

WHILE PRINCE SCRUBBED THE BASIN of the stainless-steel sink, thinking about all the events that had transpired that day, he had a feeling it was going to be another sleepless night. After leaving Vlad's house, he drove Kat to Nadia's apartment and suddenly found himself cleaning the kitchen.

Prince didn't clean.

Ever.

But it gave him a reason to stay longer since that scoundrel was still on the loose. While Kat was a competent fighter who could take care of herself, Prince found himself battling instincts he'd never felt for another woman. The desire to protect her took over all sense of reason. In any other situation he might have hired one of his men to watch over her, but this was something he couldn't walk away from. At first he thought it had to do with her being Alex's daughter, yet that didn't explain why his wolf stirred in her presence.

Being near Kat was intoxicating. Her feminine scent. Her confident voice. Her alpha temperament that made her capable and fearsome. And most especially… her candor.

A warm breath skated across his left arm. "If that sink gets any cleaner, I might take a bath in there."

He set down the scrubbing brush and looked over his shoulder at Kat. "It's the least I can do for the inconvenience I've caused your sister."

"I'm the inconvenience. You haven't done anything to deserve shining her garbage disposal."

He turned and leaned against the counter. "Our dinner was not up to her expectations."

"Because of me."

"I haven't spent as much time with her as I should have."

"Because of me."

Prince brushed a lock of hair away from her face, admiring her gentle features. "Why are you so eager to take all the blame?"

She shrugged and tucked her hands beneath her armpits. "It's just easier that way. You shouldn't have to apologize for something that's not your fault. If she's going to hate someone in this scenario, let her hate me so you're off the hook. Anyhow, you're going about it all wrong."

He inclined his head, amused by the last statement. "And how is that?"

She motioned toward the sink and lowered her arms. "Nadia doesn't care if you make her toilet and sink sparkle. She wants devotion, not servility. Most of the guys treat her good at first, but then it's all downhill. Every girl wants to be a princess, but she has a warped sense of reality and expects no less. I think what she *really* needs is someone who'll see past all that—who can get her to open up. But she thinks devotion is a man at her beck and call. If she asks you to take out her trash, tell her no. Then kiss her neck and suggest a rooftop dinner or something fancy. There's a difference between devotion and obedience, and a woman will never respect a man who isn't her equal."

He sighed and looked around at the immaculate kitchen. "You're giving me advice in love?"

"Maybe I don't know anything about it firsthand, but I thought I'd give you the inside scoop. No charge. I understand Nadia better than anyone, and I know what she wants even if she doesn't."

He stepped closer and placed his hand on her shoulder. Kat's expression softened, and she gave him a guarded look. "And you would have no qualms about me pursuing your sister?"

"If… if it's what you want."

Had he only imagined the heat between them? "Your face looks better," he said tenderly, caressing his knuckles against her cheek.

"I shifted in the bathroom."

Prince stepped closer and leaned down, whispering in her ear. "If any man ever harms you again, I'll disembowel him."

Her body hummed beneath his touch, and he remembered their brief kiss before she'd blacked out. Did she remember it?

"How old are you?" she whispered.

"Ancient. I'll live many more centuries to come."

"Did you have loving parents?"

No one had ever asked about his mother and father. His cheek brushed against hers, moving lower—his mouth grazing across her smooth skin as he drew in her scent.

In such close proximity, he became aware of her flattering shirt. Her breasts took on a more rounded shape as they pressed to his chest, and in the silence of the room, the only sound was her unsteady breath. Kat was tall for a woman, but still fell short of Prince's stature. She was tall enough for him to place a kiss to her forehead without hunching down to meet her, but it seemed like she was standing on the tips of her toes to make up the difference. Her power overwhelmed him, and when her liquid brown eyes met with his, primal heat began to flood his veins, reaching every extremity before awakening his ancient heart…

"I'm home!" Nadia announced, keys jingling and landing on a flat surface.

Kat swiftly moved away, her cheeks aflame and eyes downcast. She lightly touched the spot where his mouth had been and then turned around. "Hey. We were just… cleaning."

"And what were you cleaning in my pristine apartment?" Nadia stood in the open doorway. "Please tell me you didn't make a Packmaster scrub my kitchen floor." She turned her attention to Prince and approached with a sultry swing of her hips. "I wasn't expecting you to be here this evening. To what do I owe this pleasure?"

Kat gave him a loaded glance.

"I owe you dinner," he replied smoothly.

"Perfect. I'm starving. Where are we going?" Nadia reached out and held his hand.

Kat backed up until she met with the sink. She picked up the scrubber and played with the bristles, lifting her eyes just a fraction toward them.

"Candlelight dinner on a rooftop? It's the least I can do to smooth things over."

Nadia glanced down at her green skirt. "Should I change?"

"If it gets chilly, you can come back down for—"

"Wait a minute," she said, flipping back her blond hair. "You don't mean *my* roof, do you? I'm *not* eating on the roof of my apartment. What kind of woman do you take me for? Tell me you're only teasing."

Prince flicked his eyes between Nadia and Kat. He hadn't planned on leaving Kat alone, and it was too awkward to invite her along. Insulting Nadia by canceling his offer would displease Kat. Yet the way Kat's lips were thinning, he wasn't sure if going on the date was going to make her any happier.

"I'm beat," Kat announced, pushing away from the counter. "I think I'll go to bed early."

"It's not even dark," Nadia said. "The night is young. Why don't you see what Austin has to offer and watch a few live bands? If you'd rather go to a more upscale club, I can make a call and get you into the VIP room. This city comes to life at night."

"That's not my thing," Kat said, staring down at her sneakers.

When Nadia gave her a restrained scowl, Prince realized she was intentionally trying to get Kat out of the house.

It didn't take long for Kat to pick up on it either. "Fine. Smoky air sounds perfect. What time should I be back, sis?"

Nadia looked at her gold watch and wound it up. "Anytime after one."

"In the morning?"

"Two sounds better."

Kat waved her hand and stormed out of the room. "Fine. You two have an amazing night full of hot animal sex while I'm snacking on peanuts and napping on crusty sofas."

Prince belted out a laugh and quickly covered it before he stirred up more trouble between the twins. Nadia raked him over with a cold stare, but Prince found jealousy to be a surprisingly attractive quality in a woman, and seeing it flare up in Kat was confirmation that she wanted him for herself. But why would she give up something she wanted for her sister's happiness?

Nadia pinched the hem of Prince's T-shirt, stretching the fabric across his broad chest. "This is nice. Did you say we'd be traveling by helicopter?"

———⇒∘᝗∘⇐———

Prince needed to execute this dinner with precision. After all, it had been he who had pursued Nadia from the start, so he had an obligation to follow through with an uninterrupted date. He'd spent more time with her twin, and that riddled him with guilt because Nadia deserved a chance. So Prince had made a call and arranged for a candlelight dinner on a secluded rooftop downtown.

Dinner on a rooftop? He wished Kat had never put the thought in his head. Prince's men made a valiant effort to meet his expectations, and it had taken him an hour to locate a helicopter pilot who was available. His men had set up a cloth-covered table, silver platters, and hurricane lamps with electric candles to withstand the wind. But for him, there was nothing less romantic than eating on top of a concrete building with ventilation systems scattered about and a perilous drop just a few feet away. Perhaps there were buildings with rooftop bars and swimming pools, but this was short notice and they needed privacy.

He pulled out the wooden chair and Nadia sat down, the strong wind blowing her hair to the left. Her smile never faltered as she pulled her hair away from her face. Some strands got tangled up in her long lashes and she gracefully tucked them behind her ear. A car horn blared from the busy street below.

"Let me pour you some wine." He quickly filled their glasses before the wind blew the glassware over. "This is like eating with your head sticking out of a car window," he muttered.

"I'm sorry, I didn't hear you?"

"You look stunning beneath the moonlight."

The wind died down, thank the gods.

Nadia lifted the silver dome from her plate, then devoured the salad with her eyes. "This is perfect. I'm always watching my figure."

Prince admired Nadia's manners. Despite the harsh wind, she didn't belittle his efforts to impress her. It was strange how she mirrored Kat, but where they differed the most was in the eyes. There was something uniquely different about the way each of them looked at him, and Prince was confident he'd be able to tell them apart by their eyes alone.

"I'm going to assume you've deduced I was with your sister today."

She crunched on a radish, a faraway look in her eyes as she watched a twinkling star in the east. "I thought as much. It's just like Katarina to act so impulsively. She's living in a fantasy world where our father will be found alive and rescued, but this isn't a fairy tale. Men disappear every day and are never seen again. I've come to terms with accepting his absence, but Katarina will never move on with her life until she can do the same. The past is what holds her back from the future."

Prince cut into his salad, slicing a cherry tomato in two. "Maybe the reason she searches for her father is because that's where she received unconditional love. Siblings tend to be more critical of one another. I'm sure a woman like Kat isn't easy for you to understand, but what she needs is someone to fill his absence. Whether she finds him or not, you're her family and she seeks your approval."

Nadia gave a close-lipped laugh and gulped down her red wine. "Kat was put on this earth to make my life hell. She robbed me of my father's affection, and now you're suggesting I give her more? What makes her so special that she deserves more love than I do?"

Kat might have seemed in need of her sister's affections, but in truth, it was Kat who did everything for Nadia to show her devotion. She called, visited, and fumbled at attempts to do things for Nadia. And where was she now? She'd stepped away from a man she was interested in so her sister could be happy. Kat was sitting in a club—the last place she liked spending her free time—so that Nadia could have the apartment alone with Prince. He had seen the love for her sister shining in Kat's eyes, and all she wanted in return was the same. Yet Nadia withheld that love because of sibling rivalry, jealousy, and all the things attached to family. That's what happens when you can only see from one side of the mirror.

It had taken years for Prince to learn this for himself, and Nadia reminded him of his younger self. As the firstborn, he'd inherited land from his parents, who had even named him Prince in their language. His brother grew jealous and branched away from the family, fighting in battles to prove himself a worthy man. But his warrior status didn't impress their parents. Prince had secretly admired him, but because he never revealed this to Emil, the brothers grew distant. Prince chose to focus on the negative and, like his parents, expected his brother to become more like him. He'd hoped Emil would be his second-in-command one day, but his brother didn't want to follow in his shadow.

When Prince received news of his death, it affected him profoundly, leaving him guilt-stricken. Maybe that's why he wanted to rectify the animosity blooming between these two sisters before they met the same fate. Kat's need for acceptance from her own flesh and blood reminded him so much of Emil, to the point it unnerved him.

He set down his silver fork and centered his gaze on Nadia. "No matter what you think of her, Kat is all you have left. Time changes, money comes and goes, but she's the only person you can depend on. She'd die for you, and I'm certain you'd do the same for her if it came down to it. Accept who Kat's become, and that love might be enough to draw out the venom coursing in her veins—the poison that turns to spite."

Nadia finished her salad and gazed toward the lights twinkling below. "You've only just become acquainted with my sister; it's premature to make such assumptions. Kat is beyond my help. I've tried to get her a job, but she resists."

"You'll have to accept that she doesn't want to live the same life as you, and right now, she doesn't feel like she's good enough in your eyes."

"Since when did you become an advocate for my sister? I have no interest in discussing Katarina all evening," she said in a bored voice.

He reached across the table and held her hand, embarrassed by his lack of manners. "I apologize; that wasn't fair of me. Tell me about yourself."

"You know about my job."

"Yes, but what are your passions?"

She looked at him wolfishly and stood up from the table, approaching him from the right. The warm summer wind caressed his face, and he closed his eyes when her delicate fingers stroked his jaw. "My passion is right here."

"I mean, what is it you like to do? What are your opinions about art or—"

"I buy and sell art all day. Let's not talk about art."

Prince shifted in his chair, growing flustered. "I'm not asking to have a discussion on Picasso or black holes; I just want to know more about who you are."

Nadia leaned against the edge of the table, the wind in her favor as it picked up the silky tendrils of her long mane. It gave him a prominent view of her regal features, slender neck, lush lips, and feminine curves. He wished he had asked her to change into a pair of slacks before they left, because her sitting on the edge of the table in a skirt with her legs slightly open was testing his character as a gentleman.

"I work long hours and spend most of the day scheduling meetings and negotiating prices with my clients. I'm independent and don't need a man to take care of me. This town is alive with music, food, and people, and I like socializing with men and women. I don't like talking about myself as much as what the air smells like in Greece or why humans spend so much money trying to extend their life but a few years. I'm not sure how I feel about being mated; there's an expectation that comes with living in a pack, and I have no intention of changing my lifestyle. The right man has to come along, one who will understand my needs."

He leaned back in his chair. "But that is *all* I know about you,

Nadia. What are your real feelings about eating on a rooftop? Tell me more about where you grew up."

She reached for his glass and sipped his wine. "You're one of those talkers, aren't you? Don't you get bored talking about the same things after centuries? I have no wish to talk about the atrocities being committed against Shifters, and I don't think my childhood stories are going to change the way you feel about me." She lifted his hand and placed it on her thigh. "There are things I'd like to try on a rooftop, Prince. Show me how much you're interested. I must know if there's something between us."

"What more can I do?"

"Kiss me."

CHAPTER 9

K AT HAD NO INTENTION OF going to a stinky club and having some sweaty Shifter paw all over her. Instead, she hopped in her yellow car and tailed Prince and Nadia. She knew just how to maneuver her car so they wouldn't get away. After all, she'd probably staked out roughly three hundred outlaws, although this was her first time chasing a helicopter. The only person who'd ever gotten away from her had plowed through an intersection and struck a Labrador. Kat's little heart had melted when she saw it happen, so she'd pulled her car over and held the pup in her arms for all of thirty seconds before he had a seizure and died. After that, Kat vowed if anyone hurt an animal in her presence again, he was going to get a dagger in the balls.

So there she was—standing outside a hotel, watching her sister circle overhead in a helicopter. Kat waltzed into the hotel as if she owned the place and took the elevator. When she got near the top, she changed over to the stairs and began climbing the rest of the way. Sweat trickled down her forehead, and she panted.

"You are so out of shape," she chided, her voice reverberating off the walls. "Six tacos? *Great* way to impress a guy. Not just any guy, but a Packmaster. Nadia gets a rooftop romance with porterhouse steak, and all you have to show him is questionable meat at a roadside stand. No wonder you're still single." Kat tried to swallow, but her throat was too dry from the heavy breathing.

When she reached the top, she opened the door to the roof, then stepped into a small room and approached the outside door, but it was locked. Some places did that to keep all the crazies from going up there and jumping to their death. But Kat knew how to pick a lock, so she knelt down and caught her breath while fiddling with the mechanism.

"*Fly me to the moon*," she sang, continuing the lyrics until the door unlocked. She tucked her handy little tool back in its pouch and slowly eased the door open. "*Please be true*," she whispered more than sang.

The door cracked open a few inches, and when Kat beheld the enchanting scene before her, she took a seat on the cold concrete. Despite the wind whipping the white tablecloth at the bottom, the candles remained lit inside their colored lanterns. Nadia looked like Aphrodite with her hair blowing in the breeze like ribbons of silk. Prince was doing most of the talking, which struck her as odd because he was always the quiet one around her.

"God, maybe I *do* have a big mouth," she remarked.

Kat looked on with a rueful heart, wondering if she'd made the right decision in letting them go without an objection. It wasn't as if Prince would take her seriously since clearly the better half was currently sitting opposite him, but it didn't eliminate the sting in knowing she hadn't even put up a fight. Then again, what would her father have thought if she'd ruined her relationship with Nadia over the affections of a man?

She rested her head against the doorjamb when Prince reached across the table and held Nadia's hand.

Kat was close to her father for the same reason her twin had been close with their mother. Nadia was like a little clone, and in some ways, she'd grown up to become just like their mother. As a little girl, Kat had envied the special affection that her mother had shown her sister, so she understood how Nadia must have felt regarding Kat's close relationship with their father. Both sisters were dealt a bad hand when they lost both parents, but at least Nadia had managed to get her life into some semblance of normalcy.

Stars glittered above, moonlight illuminated the picturesque scene, and Nadia rose from her chair. It was almost too painful to watch as she rounded the table and stood before the alpha. Kat hadn't known Prince very long, but being with him was easy and comfortable, like the jeans she had on.

When Nadia cupped his face and leaned down, Kat realized why they put locks on roof doors. She stared for a frozen moment and then looked away, an unfamiliar pain gripping her chest. Kat didn't feel jealous; she felt wounded.

The kiss always sealed the deal. Men couldn't resist Nadia once they got a taste. *She must be a phenomenal kisser*, Kat thought. Not that Kat lacked skills of her own, but she just hadn't had as much practice.

After a moment, Kat glanced up, and her eyes widened in horror. A man approached the table—just a slithering shadow that appeared out of nowhere.

"*Vlad*."

He must have used his Mage gift to jump from the nearby building.

Kat flung the door open, and it became one of those intense scenes that played out in slow motion in her head, like a *Die Hard* movie. She moved like a torpedo, her feet pounding against the hard surface, her hands pulled into tight fists, energy rolling off her, the wind blowing her hair back. Nadia had leaned down to kiss Prince, both of them unaware that Vlad had eased up behind them, a malicious grin widening on his face as he sharpened his light.

Kat dove through the air and crashed on top of the table. As it toppled over, plates broke and silverware clattered against the concrete. When the table rolled slightly to the side, the tablecloth blew off into the night. She flipped onto her back and scanned the roof, but Vlad was nowhere to be seen.

Nadia and Prince stared down at her, aghast. A cherry tomato rolled by, and lettuce covered the entire scene like a produce massacre.

"You just couldn't let me have *one* night," Nadia said gruffly, hands on hips. "Why must you always ruin everything?"

Kat lifted the bottle of wine and handed it to Nadia. "At least the wine didn't break?"

Prince rocked with laughter and covered his eyes, stopping his outburst before Nadia looked daggers at him.

When her sister didn't take the bottle, Kat took a swig.

Vlad was messing with her head. She hoped like hell he didn't know anything about Nadia being related to their father. If he somehow already knew that Alex had twin daughters, then maybe Nadia's blond hair threw him off. But when Kat replayed the scene in her head, it seemed like Vlad had been going after Prince. He might have assumed Prince meant something to Kat, and after crashing his house earlier, it wouldn't surprise her if Vlad was on the warpath for revenge. Maybe he found out she'd stolen sensitive information from his computer, or maybe he didn't like the way she'd poured all his beer into the toilet.

"I think I've had enough excitement for one evening," Nadia announced, wiping at a splash of red wine that had stained her short skirt.

"I won't be able to get the chopper back for another hour," Prince said, glancing at his naked wrist and then realizing he didn't have on a watch. Just that nice body-hugging T-shirt that showed off his taut muscles.

Which made Kat take another swig before humming "Bad Moon Rising."

Nadia offered her hand to Prince. "Let's go."

He stood up and looked down at Kat. "Do you think we should leave her in this condition?"

Well, *that* was embarrassing. Either Prince thought she was a lunatic or a drunk. Kat leaned back against the short wall along the edge of the building, soaking in the humiliation. Sure, she could have revealed why she'd taken down the table like a bridesmaid diving for a bouquet, but what were the odds of them believing her? Didn't matter. As long as they went straight home, Kat was fine with being the delusional sister for the evening. Nadia's apartment was safer than the roof of a building downtown. More than half her complex was Breed, so they usually kept an eye on things.

Prince sent a text message and turned to Nadia. "One of my men will escort you home. Your sister's in no condition to operate a vehicle, so I'll bring her back safely."

Swell. He thinks I'm an alcoholic, Kat thought with amusement. Especially humorous since they'd drank half the bottle and she'd only taken two sips.

Nadia shook her head and touched his arm. "You should be sainted."

Kat climbed onto the wall and swung her legs over the edge, listening to the hard click of high heels growing distant.

Strong hands gripped her shoulders. "Hey, this is dangerous. You might fall."

She patted the spot to her left. "Live on the edge, Charming. You get a whole new perspective on life from this seat versus the one behind you."

Prince straddled the wall and gingerly lifted one of his long legs over the edge, leaning back at first, then peering down with curiosity at the twinkling lights below.

"What are we looking at?" he asked.

She handed him the bottle of Italian wine and pointed at the smaller building across from them. "Vlad was here. He must have jumped over from that rooftop and was moving in on you guys when you were about to lock lips."

Kat could feel the intensity of his gaze as he studied her.

"Sorry I ruined your dinner. Again," she said, still looking at the building in front of them. "It was either that or watch you guys take an unplanned free fall. He's messing with my head. I don't think he knows Nadia is related to me, or I'm positive he would have gone through with it. He probably thinks she's just one of your floozies." Kat snorted and then snatched the wine when she noticed he wasn't drinking it.

"Vlad is a man who doesn't give empty threats. If he was here on this roof, then he meant to go through with something. Had you not intervened, he would have taken us by complete surprise. I don't believe he was taunting you. He wouldn't have been able to fight all three of us, and he's just the sort of man who would rather stab someone in the back than fight with honor."

"I'm such an idiot," she said under her breath. "I led him right to you."

A gust of wind blew from behind, and Kat leaned back to keep her balance. Prince did the same and made no attempt to get up. In fact, he tilted his head back and closed his eyes, an indefinable expression painted on his handsome face. A look that was relaxed and introspective, and she stole a private moment to admire his profile. She was drawn to his confident nature, and yet she couldn't help but notice a hint of sadness beneath it all.

"This is nice," he said. "I've never sat on the edge of a building. People would find it foolish for someone with my responsibilities to be so impetuous."

His leg brushed against her knee and it gave her butterflies. Katarina Kozlov—bounty hunter—felt a flutter in her tummy over a man.

"Being important sounds like a drag. You're so busy trying to do the right thing that you don't actually do the stuff that matters."

"Sitting inches from death matters?"

Kat set the bottle down behind her. "Sure. Sometimes you have to get close to the edge to remind yourself what life's about. It's not just about rules or what's on TV tonight. It's about taking a second to look up and admire the universe." They both simultaneously glanced up at the sky. "It's about taking a deep breath and listening to the sounds of life. Maybe it sounds corny to you, but it's how I get past all the drama with Nadia. I just sit back and remember that this won't last and how thankful I am that she's in my life. Sitting on the edge reminds me that someday I'm going to be nothing more than a handful of dust, so I need to make the most of every opportunity. The only way to live life is to live in the present. You can't put things off thinking you'll have time later. There may not *be* a later."

Right there, on the ledge of a building with stars above and city streets below, Prince leaned over and kissed her. The moment their lips touched, the entire world melted away, and it felt as if they had been lifted by the wind and embraced by the stars. His tongue met with hers—insistent and experienced. Nothing about his kiss was clumsy or hurried, and it was as if they'd been lovers for centuries.

Kat reached up and pulled the band out of his hair so she could run her fingers through it. He moaned against her mouth, kissing her harder, and her body pulsed with need. When she peeked through her lashes at him, his brows were drawn together in a slant—an intense look that was so hot she shut her eyes and kissed him harder.

She drew closer to him as he slid his hand around her lower back, and all she could think about was the stupid flannel shirt creating a barrier between his palm and her flesh.

When she nibbled on his lip, he pulled back.

"Wait," he said with a throaty growl.

She glanced down and noticed he was holding her right thigh with a forceful grip. *Oops.* Kat had gotten so carried away that she'd tried to straddle him.

On the ledge of a high-rise building.

Tripping over her feet was one thing, but plummeting to her death while making out with a Packmaster was something entirely different.

His charismatic smile made a graceful appearance, and Kat couldn't help but notice that Prince looked like a different man with his hair down. There wasn't enough light to see the differences in his eye color, only to notice how they lit up when he looked at her. "You're one of a kind."

Kat's heart clenched. No one had ever said romantic words to her—not like that. *One of a kind* was the best kind of compliment given she was an identical twin. "Why are you so nice to me?"

He leaned in, his warm lips against her neck, his breath heating her skin, the moon reflecting off his hair as it tangled in the wind. "I want you, Kat. My wolf sings for you whenever you're near."

Breathless, she pushed him back and swallowed hard. "You barely know me. I've almost gotten you killed. I hunt men for a living and wear a knife strapped to my chest. I talk too much. I eat like a horse and—"

"And if you keep talking, Katarina, I'm going to make love to you on this ledge. Everything about you I want. Nothing more. Nothing less. Just you as you are."

"But Nadia…"

He pressed his index finger against her lips. "She doesn't want me. She wants the idea of me."

"How do you know?"

Prince was just a breath away from her lips. "Because she doesn't look at me the way you do. I don't feel her soul staring into mine like an imprint on my existence. You're brutally honest with who you are, and I find that incredibly attractive. I have no desire to pursue your sister any further than it's gone tonight. I don't wish to mislead anyone."

"You never did tell me about your parents."

Prince kissed her feverishly, and Kat gave in, closing her eyes and slowing down until the kiss became demanding. Her body hummed with energy, and the next thing she knew, he was standing up and pulling her into his arms. The wind blew her hair to the side, but she didn't care. All she wanted were moonlight kisses.

His dark hair twisted into tousled strands, obscuring his eyes and then revealing them once more.

"Don't look at me like that," she said on a breath.

"Like what?"

Like you love me, she thought. Kat had seen that look plenty of times among mated Shifters. Courtships were so different than in the human world, and some believed in life mates, which was the equivalent of a soul mate. If that were true, then what about her father and mother? If they weren't life mates, why would they have settled?

"What are you thinking?" he asked. "I don't like it when you're quiet."

"No one's ever said that to me before." Kat smiled and broke into a soft laugh. "I just crashed on top of your dinner table and ruined your night, and now you're telling me you can't wait to see what I'll do next? I'm like one of those TV shows, Charming. Don't mix feelings of love with the thrill of watching a car chase."

His brows knitted together. "You don't understand."

"Trust me, I get it. Your life has gotten a little monotonous and safe, and I'm a carnival ride. I live a crazy life, and people are attracted to that, but the novelty wears off after a while. You're going to realize this is too much craziness for your taste, so don't declare something you're not ready for."

He encircled her waist with his strong arms, and the intense look that crossed his face frightened her. Prince had all the manners of an aristocrat, but she couldn't forget for one second that he was an ancient alpha who might revert back to barbaric ways and toss her off the building.

His gaze never wavered. "Trust me, I'm more than ready."

"You don't want this."

"Shut up, Kat."

Her eyes widened. "Did you just tell me to shut up?"

"Yep."

She hooked her right leg around his. "Ooo, I love it when you speak like the commoners."

She kissed his neck and relished the feel of his whiskers against her lips. "You're vibrating," she whispered.

"Mmm, yes."

Kat stepped back. "No, your phone. It's vibrating."

Prince pulled his phone out of his pocket, a look of annoyance on his face. "Yes?"

While he answered, she lifted the fallen table and set it right, whispering to herself, "Kat, you have completely lost your mind." She briefly eyed the small cakes and wondered if the five-second rule applied on a rooftop. Although five seconds had already elapsed into five minutes.

When she looked over her shoulder at Prince, he was frozen beneath a shower of moonlight, his dark hair rippling in the wind. He held the phone at his side, and an emotion flickered in his eyes that sent a shiver down her spine.

Kat pivoted around and closed the distance between them, her heart beating in double time. "What's wrong?"

Prince kept his eyes on the shattered plates, his voice gruff. "There was an ambush." After what seemed like an eternity of silence, his eyes dragged up to meet hers. "Nadia was taken."

Emotions erupted so suddenly that she couldn't contain the sorrow and rage swirling together like an imminent storm. Kat lifted the wine bottle and hurled it so violently that it smashed on the neighboring rooftop.

"*I'll kill you, Vlad!*" she screamed into the void. "Do you hear me? You're dead!"

Prince wouldn't allow Kat to drive in her emotional state. She was livid and liable to wreck the car. They arrived at Nadia's apartment at lightning speed, staying long enough to grab the flash drive and some other items Kat wanted.

It wasn't safe to remain there, so Prince left the city and drove them to his mansion. Despite the late hour, neither of them was tired. Kat was despondent, so he didn't pressure her to talk. The guard opened the main gate, which stood almost twenty feet high. Prince parked on the right side, and they entered the house through the breezeway. Once inside, Kat stalked through the rotunda toward the back of the house without saying a word, oblivious to her lavish surroundings, her stride angry as she disappeared around the corner.

"Sire," Russell said, bowing respectfully. He had on a tight-fitted white shirt with dark suspenders. It was a look that had always amused Prince, but the situation was far too grim for such humorous distractions.

"What happened?" Prince demanded.

His Scottish packmate was still sporting fresh injuries to his face and lip. "A Mage slammed into my motor when we crossed an intersection. I thought he was hammered, but then he pulled the woman out. I had to crawl through an open window to go after him. The shitebag knocked me unconscious with a blast of energy, and when I woke up, he was gone."

"And Nadia? Was she injured?" Anger ripped through Prince like a streak of lightning, and it took everything in his power not to shift. Nadia didn't deserve this.

"Probably took a hit to her noggin, but she's not dead."

Prince traced his finger across his eyebrow, trying to dissect what Vlad was up to by kidnapping Nadia. He couldn't have known she was Kat's twin since he had only seen her from behind on the rooftop.

"Why didn't you shift and heal?" Prince asked, looking at the cut on Russell's hand.

His beta pulled a few pieces of glass from his unruly hair. "I deserve what I got, and I'll keep the scars as a reminder."

Prince respected him for taking accountability. "Did you see what the car looked like?"

"The license plate is burned into my brain," he gritted out.

"Good. I want you to pay a visit to the man I think was behind this. Tell me if the car on the property matches the plates. I need to know if he was foolish enough to return home or if he's gone into hiding."

Russell clenched his fists until his knuckles turned white. "What's the bastard's name?"

"Vladimir Romanov. I've looked through his file, but I want you to speak to your contacts and see what else you can find out."

Prince looked past Russell at Kat strutting into the room, tearing off a strip of meat from a barbecue rib with her teeth.

"I couldn't find a microwave," she said unapologetically.

Russell turned around and said, "We don't have one."

Kat waved the bone at Prince, and he sensed the fire in her had returned. "Christmas wish list. So what's the plan? I need a plan, Charming. I can't just sit here waiting for him to call—*if* he calls. He's got my sister."

"Your sister?" Russell asked, stepping forward. "Aye, I can see the resemblance. She's a bonnie lass, but you don't have her flaxen hair and comely smile."

Kat narrowed her eyes at him. "I don't think we've been introduced."

Prince moved between them. "Russell, this is Katarina Kozlov, my close companion."

They both turned their eyes to Prince, but he didn't retract the declaration.

"And how close is a *close companion*?" Russell asked, his green eyes glittering with interest.

"Kat, this is Russell Stover, one of my most loyal packmates and second-in-command."

Kat snorted and licked a dab of sauce from her hand. The sight of her wet tongue made Prince shift his stance.

"Your name is Russell Stover?"

"My father was half-German," he said matter-of-factly.

"What's that supposed to mean?"

"He had a remarkable sense of humor."

Kat blinked and looked him over. "I don't even get that."

"Course you wouldn't, being that you're Russian."

"Hey, we're funny. My Russian roots are freaking hilarious," Kat said, waving her rib.

"Aye," Russell agreed, strolling upstairs. "That cold war had me in stitches for a decade."

Prince covered his eyes and suppressed his laughter.

Kat gave him a peevish glance. "Well, I'm glad someone around here has a sense of humor."

He took the rib from her hand and tossed it at one of the wolves guarding the main room. "You remind me so much of your father."

For the first time, Kat broke down. Her knees almost buckled as she fell against Prince, her arms encircling his broad chest and her tears wetting his thin shirt. He breathed in her scent, whispering words of comfort in Russian.

"We'll find your father and sister. You have my promise."

She shook her head against his chest. "I can't lose her. Nadia's all I have left. She has nothing to do with this. It should have been me."

"Kat, look at me." He cradled her head and forced her to look up. "I won't allow this bastard to harm your family."

"Promise?"

Prince didn't think it was a promise he could keep, not if Vlad was on the move. He'd hunt him down for as long as it took and tear him to pieces when caught, but a promise like that could destroy her trust in him.

"Russell!" he shouted at the ceiling.

Within seconds, his packmate appeared halfway down the curved staircase. "I'm not done yet."

"Put out a bulletin to all the packs in the territory. Give them the car description and license plate. I want them alive, and no one is to harm the woman. Offer a substantial reward. Contact my allies in all directions near major highways. I want them to create diversions and slow traffic down enough to check out the vehicles. I don't want Vlad leaving the city limits. And do me a favor... have someone drive to Nadia Kozlov's apartment and retrieve the yellow car out front. Same address I provided you for the helicopter."

"Right away," Russell said, running up the stairs.

Kat backed away from Prince, her lashes wet. "You can do all that?"

"I have an immeasurable amount of power. Not only in this territory, brave one, but in all the Southern states."

"Thank you. That'll help a lot."

He reached up and wiped a dab of barbecue sauce off her chin. "Is your wolf hungry? Does she need to run?"

Kat nodded. "Both. But... I don't feel comfortable letting her out on your property. She doesn't know your pack."

Not an uncommon reaction for a Shifter in a stranger's house. "I have an indoor facility in the basement."

"Sounds cheery."

"I converted the entire lower level for privacy. Two feet of packed dirt with grass and plants on top. There's a woman who grows the plants with special lights and fertilizers. I think she keeps the plants potted beneath the ground to control roots, but I leave that to her."

"As long as you don't bury bodies down there, I'm game."

Prince guided her toward the stairs that led to the basement. "I can release a rabbit if you want."

"No, it's better if my wolf doesn't get blood in her mouth when I'm in this kind of mood. She's a little different than most. She'll eat cooked meat, so if you could just put some ribs or whatever you've got left over, that's what I'd rather have."

He fell back a step, overcome with an eerie sense that Kat belonged here—that what had always been missing from his home was now standing beside him.

"Whatever you wish."

CHAPTER 10

N ADIA OPENED HER EYES WHEN a familiar voice called her name.

"My Nadia, wake up."

The words spoken were in Russian, repeating the same thing.

"Papa?" She blinked through the blurriness and rolled to her side, wondering if she was still caught in a dream.

"That's right," he said, his voice husky. "I have prayed for your safety."

She sat up, her head pounding. The last thing she remembered was a car smashing into her ride and a loud explosion of metal and glass—a sound she could still hear repeating in her head like a record skipping.

"I made you shift once," he said. "Do it again if you're not all the way healed."

"No... I..." Nadia sat up and dizzily looked at her surroundings. *It all seems surreal,* she thought.

For the first time in two decades, she laid eyes on her father—a man she had laid to rest in her heart long ago in order to cope. He appeared exactly the same, only frail, as if he'd been underfed. Coarse grey hairs mixed in with the black, and his beard was much too long. Even his voice sounded as if he hadn't used it in a long time. Her heart clenched when she saw his raggedy clothes.

"*Papa.*" Nadia crawled across the concrete floor and fell into his arms, weeping uncontrollably.

"Shhh, my princess," he said, his thick accent soothing her like sweet honey. A voice she had heard in her dreams so many times. "Nadia, what have you done to your hair?"

She sat up, looking down at her blond locks. "You don't like it?"

He shrugged as fathers often do. "You were always beautiful to me. Why are you here?"

"Me? Why are *you* here? Where are we?"

He thumped the back of his head against the cinder block wall behind him. "I've been here many years—too many to count. I don't even know when it's day or night except when I'm fed, which isn't often when he's out of town and his men don't come by. There is a long history between Vladimir and me."

She lifted the chain around his feet, following the links that bolted into the wall. "But why would he do this? He's had you here this whole time?"

"There's something he wants that I won't give him, so he keeps me here out of spite, hoping one day he'll break me. But *how* did he know about *you?*"

She shook her head, not understanding.

"He did not know I had children. I convinced him I had no one, and he foolishly believed me."

Nadia realized she wasn't bound in any way. Her eyes darted around the room in search of something to break his chains. "I have to free you."

"*Nyet.* I want you to lie down and pretend you are weak and afraid. When he comes back, I'm going to wrap this chain around his neck, and you're going to escape. He's a Mage, but I can hold him back long enough for you to get out and lock us inside. Then you take his car and drive as far away as you can."

"I can't leave you here!" Tears slipped past her lashes, and she gripped a handful of his shirt.

Her father cursed in Russian and then calmed himself, asking a question that distracted her. "How is my Kat?"

"She's still a bounty hunter."

Alex smiled, and even beneath that wild beard she could see it. "That pleases me. Did you know when she first told me what she did, I made the mistake of calling her a huntress?" He laughed, his eyes sparkling with memories. "She said a profession shouldn't come with gender tags and she could do the job just as well as any man.

Kat always wanted to be a hunter like her father. And how is my princess Nadia?"

"I'm not working in that museum anymore. I'm a businesswoman, connecting buyers and sellers of valuable art," she said with a sniff.

"Always my smart girl," he said, patting her cheek lovingly.

Nadia hadn't realized how much she missed her father. She'd spent so many years trying to forget him that she'd forgotten how raw the pain of his absence was. "I didn't think you were proud of me."

His thick brows furrowed. "I have always been a proud father. My two beautiful girls—strong and intelligent. I do not love one more than the other."

"And which am I? The strong one or the intelligent one?"

Her father held up both of his hands. "You are born from the same seed and will always be stronger when you are together," he said, clasping his fingers together. "You each have strength, but different. Kat has a strong will and body, but you have an iron heart. You are smart with learning all kinds of things from books that I never understood, and Kat is cunning. She could outwit a fox."

"But all that time you spent with Katarina…"

"Nadia, my children are two halves of my heart, but you were always the one who had control over her emotions. Your mother leaving almost broke Katarina. Even though you were the one closest to your mother, Kat has always had the tender heart. That is her Achilles' heel. I have made mistakes; I was not a perfect father," he said, shaking his head. "But now you are grown women, and you must be there for each other. You can't worry about what this old man thinks."

"Oh, Papa." Nadia wrapped her arms around him and kissed his cheek.

When the door above opened, her father shoved her forcefully to the cement floor.

Footsteps approached. "What a coincidence. Of all people I bring here, it's your own flesh and blood. Why didn't you tell me long ago that you had a daughter, Alexei?" The man called Vlad stood behind Nadia, and she stayed absolutely motionless while he continued. "Silent treatment again? I don't suppose you gave her my ring as a gift, did you? We could have settled this years ago. You could have been free! But once again, I have been deceived."

Nadia tensed when her father didn't reply.

"Is that how it's going to be?" Vlad erupted. "Don't you dare shut your eyes and ignore me!"

She tried to slow down her racing heart and meanwhile noticed the most trivial things. Like she was barefoot, and her skirt was twisting painfully around her waist.

Vlad leaned forward and grabbed her father by the collar. "You are lucky to be alive. I am the only thing keeping you in this world, so you give me what is mine or else… I just might take something that's precious to *you*."

Nadia gasped when her father erupted in a violent motion and wrapped the chain around Vlad's neck.

"Run!"

Kat rolled over and nestled onto a cool patch of dirt. She glanced at her surroundings and remembered she was in a basement, despite the fact it looked more like a nature preserve at midnight. Small dim lights in the ceiling resembled scattered stars, and the main light shone from behind the man-made waterfall to her right, which was nothing more than water cascading down a rock wall.

"How long was I out?"

Prince was sitting on a flat rock a few feet in front of her. He scratched his bristly jaw, his hair still loose and maddeningly sexy. "Your wolf was out for maybe two hours. She especially enjoyed the rare steak I brought down for her."

Steak? Kat highly doubted those were leftovers in his fridge— not in a pack full of wolves. Prince had cooked for her wolf and fed her, and did *that* ever stir a primal feeling of desire in her. That was almost as good as hunting for her animal, although no Shifter had ever done that before.

Prince smiled with his warm, generous eyes. "She's a beautiful creature."

"Any news?"

"I haven't heard from Vlad, but he's not getting out of this city without my knowing. It won't take long to track him down; we just need to rest and wait for news."

She stretched out on her side, loving the feel of her nude body against cool earth. "This is a nice place. I felt safe in here."

"It comes in handy," he said, his eyes skating down the length of her body and then flicking away.

Her nudity shouldn't have fazed him, but he was taking pleasure from small glimpses. Kat's pulse quickened, especially when he leaned forward, showing off his taut muscles.

She felt a renewed vigor, as if her wolf had erased the anxiety of Nadia's abduction and helped her to refocus. In the morning, she would make plans and come up with a strategy, but for tonight... Her heart sank when images of Nadia flashed in her mind. Did she have a warm blanket? Was she being brave, confident her sister would find her?

Prince's voice became tender, as if he could read her mind and wanted to create the distraction she so desperately needed. "What is it you crave and I'll bring it down?"

All Shifters came out of their shift craving a specific food unique to them. It was the worst kind of desire and hunger pang all at once, but tolerable.

She smiled and stretched again. "Unless you feel like cooking up some french toast with powdered sugar and syrup, I'm fine. I bet you crave something easy like tomato soup."

Kat looked down at Prince's bare feet, planted on the dirt, toes digging in.

"Actually, my craving is potatoes."

Her brows popped up. "That's unusual, and a little bit sad."

"Yes, and not always something we have in the house. I can't eat any of the packaged or canned foods. It has to be fresh."

"Maybe you should make some soup out of it and hide it in the freezer."

He looked down at her thoughtfully before lowering to all fours, crawling across the dirt like a predator.

Kat shivered and rolled onto her back, looking up at him. "What did I say?"

His blue and brown eyes leisurely made their way down to the curve of her hips, her sex, her long legs. "I like the way you want to take care of me."

Kat bit her lip. Whether she hunted for him or vice versa, feeding a Shifter had many meanings. Offering food to someone in your house was a sign of trust, but with the opposite sex, it could be seen as a sign of loyalty and devotion. She wasn't sure how devoted she could be to a man she'd just met, but when he stripped out of his T-shirt and revealed a resplendent physique, she decided not to rule out the possibility that the fates wanted her to share her body with this man.

"I'm going to lie with you, Kat," he said, his voice silken as he unbuttoned his jeans.

Desire pulsed through her, as if every emotion she was feeling needed this union—this release.

She reached out, dragging his pants and briefs down his hips as he sucked in a sharp breath. Kat ran her hand along his strong back from his shoulder blades down to his firm ass while he kicked out of his clothes. She preferred strong arms and hands, but she gave his ass a hard squeeze and watched his eyes smolder.

They each lay on their sides, facing each other. The dim light made it feel as though they could have been outside, lying together on sacred Shifter land where no one would discover them. The walls were painted like a forest, and the ceiling was midnight black. All they lacked was a warm wind and the sound of crickets chirping.

As much as she wanted to feel his body against hers, she traced her finger over the coarse stubble on his jaw, across his collarbone, along the grooves of his ribs, and down to his belly button, avoiding the obvious elephant in the room that was swinging his rather large trunk. Kat adored being able to admire a man's body and take it all in, as he did with hers. Every touch elicited a reaction, and his natural scent became stronger, mingled with earth and greenery.

Prince stroked her like a precious thing, resting his hand on the dip in her waist. "You're exquisite."

"And a little dirty," she said with an impish grin. "Are you sure you don't want to go upstairs and do this on silken sheets with golden bedposts to hold on to?"

He moved in close, his body hot to the touch. "This is the true Shifter way," he growled under his breath. "This is the way we did it hundreds of years ago—nothing but two bodies finding bliss on the soft bed of earth." His mouth dragged to her ear and whispered, "Open your legs, Kat."

She gasped when his fingers slipped between her thighs and stroked the silken crease of her sex. The sharp arousal made her moan, and she put her left arm over his shoulder and parted her legs for him like an obedient wolf.

"Like silk," he said on a soft breath.

Pleasure ripped through her with his feather-soft strokes. His ravenous eyes were no longer on her body, but staring straight into her soul. A hunger burned in those irises, intensifying each time she gasped and arched her body beneath his touch.

"I want to do this the old way," he said, his voice rough and sexy.

Kat knew little about the mating rituals of the ancients outside the fact that they were experienced lovers.

"Is that different?" she asked, writhing beneath his rhythmic strokes. Heat flushed her skin, contrasting with the cool earth against her side.

"The old way among my tribe involved little foreplay. Just pleasure. Screams of pleasure."

"Sounds like my kind of party," she said, then found herself trembling with anticipation when he didn't smile back.

Kat wasn't used to giving up her dominance in the bedroom, and it excited her. This was a man who killed his adversaries without remorse, an alpha with enough power to create a kingdom if he so desired. She could feel the intensity of his energy rolling off him like ripples of water against the shore.

Prince pulled his hand away. "Take me inside your mouth." He hesitated, perhaps wondering if his bold statement might offend her.

Kat wasn't easily offended. She nuzzled into his neck and whispered, "Yummy," inciting a groan from deep within his chest.

She scooted down, leaving a pit in the dirt where her body once lay. When she reached his hips, she circled her tongue around the tip of his erection.

Prince tightened his fingers in her hair, and she felt him shaking with anticipation. "No, not like that. All the way. Deep. I want you to get it wet."

Kat licked her lips, looking up at him. His breathing grew heavy and his eyes blazed with primal heat. She opened her mouth and took him in as far as she could, then pulled back slowly, wetting the length of him.

In a motion too fast to track, Prince flipped her onto her stomach and slid deep into her core. He held her hands and rocked into her—nothing like she'd ever experienced. His moves were sudden and animalistic.

Prince had found a striking point within her that intensified so quickly, she realized it was leading her to orgasm far sooner than she wanted.

"Do you feel that?" he asked. "Right *there*."

A lick of pleasure rippled through her, just a taste of what was to come. Kat was breathing so fast that dirt blew in front of her face. Her fingers clawed into the earth, and instinct told her to widen her legs instead of rising up on her knees. A coil of need tightened between her legs, and nothing he did was enough to sate that desire.

"*Yes,*" he hissed, quickening his thrusts.

"Not yet! Charming…" She was embarrassed at how determined he was to make her come and how easy the task seemed to be.

He pounded harder. "Release your inhibitions and give in to your instincts. Your wolf knows she's with a pureblood. The heat will take you first."

This was like nothing she'd ever experienced. *What kind of ancient was he?* Liquid heat surged through her body, and she trembled at its power. Her wolf was on the cusp of coming out—but not. The Shifter magic within them swirled and spiraled into a heavenly oblivion.

The provocative sounds he made were a mixture of growls and ancient words she didn't understand. The man who cared about appearances and rules now had his elbows in the dirt, cursing as she moaned beneath him.

"Oh God, what's happening?" She gasped, feeling an unexpected pressure.

He kissed her neck, a current of possession resonating in his tone as he slowed. "I'm not just an ancient, Kat. I'm from a powerful line of purebloods. I'm going to get bigger, so I need you to relax and trust me. You feel so *tight*…"

Specks of light flashed before her eyes and her muscles tensed. Prince's shaft felt twice the size around as it had been when they started, and my God, she'd never felt anything so hot in all her life.

"I need more!" she demanded, lifting her hips, commanding him to go deep.

Prince roared, sitting up and grabbing onto her hips until their flesh was slapping together. And then it happened, like a Mage blasting her with energy, only ecstasy instead of pain.

Kat's body relaxed before she came. The wave took over her entire being, deep within her core and radiating down her limbs. Prince kept going and would periodically stop, then thrust deep once again. He was having multiple orgasms, and this went on for what seemed like an eternity while she continued having light flutters of her own.

They collapsed against each other, spent and wrapped together in a knot of arms and legs.

"And tell me again how it is you're not mated?" she asked with a laugh of disbelief. "Exactly what *was* that?"

He rolled onto his back and pulled her against him. "Few women have ever experienced that with me. And by few I mean only three. I always hold back."

"Why?"

He averted his eyes. "It frightens them because I'm not like other Shifters; they don't understand it. The last one tensed during the act and became so frightened it… it regretfully caused her pain. I immediately stopped, but she wasn't receptive of my explanation, and I never saw her again."

"It's not something you can help."

"The ritual is reserved for mates who trust each other. If the trust isn't there, then it can be uncomfortable. I vowed to never again let myself feel that kind of unrestrained desire for a woman, not if it meant them experiencing even a moment of discomfort. But with you—with you I feel I can be myself completely. Had you been in heat, it would have given us children."

"Well, that would have happened whether you had a superpenis or not."

A laugh burst out of his mouth, and he threw his arm over his eyes. She pulled it away, realizing Prince was uncomfortable with spontaneous laughter, as if it revealed a weakness. Perhaps he felt it wasn't permissible for a man of his authority to display an emotional reaction that could result in someone not taking him seriously as a leader. She'd seen it happen before, and maybe that was why her heart melted a little whenever she managed to draw him out of his shell.

"Pregnancy most often occurs with repeated intercourse," he said. "Most mated couples will engage throughout her cycle, increasing her odds to conceive. The temptation can hardly be helped. With someone like me, it would only take one time."

"So why isn't everyone, um… built like you?"

He put his arm behind his head, and she imagined what he must have looked like as a man living in the fourteen hundreds. "Each pureblood family had unique traits that were lost over time as they mated outside their animal or with someone who came from a Shifter family with mixed heritage anywhere in their ancestry. I suppose Mother Nature phases out things she finds unnecessary."

Kat kissed his chest and gave him an indulgent smile. "Chickens having wings is unnecessary. But that? That was *really* necessary. How about we do it my way next time?"

"I'm afraid to ask what that might involve."

Kat eased up on her elbow and brushed the dirt from her chest, but it was pointless since she looked like someone who had crawled from the bowels of the earth. "I thought you liked the unexpected?"

He placed a reverent kiss on her lips, which she felt in her soul, and it mended all the jagged rips and tears from her past. "You *are* my unexpected."

She gazed into his eyes, wondering if there was anything special about her, being that she was also a pureblood. She definitely didn't shoot bullets with her nipples, although that might have made things interesting. Perhaps her bloodline simply wasn't as pure as his.

He tapped her nose. "What are you thinking about?"

"Does it snow in Austin?" she asked, playing with the idea of settling down.

"Not often."

She traced her finger down his jaw. "Do you think your friend can get me started as a PI? Nobody around here knows me; it would be like starting over."

Prince smiled with closed lips, and she pushed the corners of his mouth a little higher. "I trust Reno will be able to help you build clientele."

"So… is this a thing?"

He flipped her onto her back and ran his tongue along her neck and up to her ear. "This is most definitely a thing, alpha female."

Kat threw her weight forward until she sat astride him, pinning his wrists to the ground. "We'll see how this plays out, but right now, I need a shower."

She stood up and strolled to the waterfall, dirt flaking off her body. There were drains in the floor to keep the room from flooding. "Your water bill must be high," she said with a snort.

"It recycles. They change it a few times a week since it's rarely used."

Kat rinsed the dirt from her skin while Prince found a patch of grass and watched her, his impressive body glistening with sweat, pieces of dirt stuck to his sides and forearms.

"This is some setup you have down here." Kat found her holster and strapped it on before getting dressed. "I don't know anybody who puts dirt in their basement unless they're a serial killer."

"I would hardly call this dirt," he said, waving an arm at his exceptional design.

Vines grew along the columns and walls, special lights were

placed to accent the grass and plants, and it was more spacious than it appeared. The main room they were in walled off an adjoining room that had an obstacle course for their wolves to leap on and around.

Except for alphas, most Shifters blacked out shortly after their animal took over the shift, and thank God for that. Her wolf was a separate spirit connected to her own, so sharing consciousness at the same time would be maddening. The only thing she didn't like was the unexpected surprises of where she wound up after a shift. Kat once woke up in a McDonald's playground.

Naked.

So having an indoor facility for the wolves was pretty ingenious.

Those thoughts faded as she put on her clothes and wondered if Nadia was okay. What the hell did Vlad want with her sister?

"Kat?"

"What?" She looked up and Prince was standing before her.

"You weren't answering."

"What does he have against my father?"

"He resents Alex for having bought his own freedom. It might have been decades in the making, but Alex outwitted Vlad in the end." After stepping beneath the water and rinsing himself clean, Prince shook out his T-shirt and pulled it over his head.

She tapped her chin. "I think my father stole something valuable of his. Vlad is behaving like a dog that's searching for his favorite toy. Men who want revenge just do it; they don't play mind games or they risk getting caught. When my father went missing, his cabin was ransacked. Vlad was looking for something."

"If Alex has it, then surely he would have given it to him by now."

"Maybe not. You said my father outwitted him after decades of patient waiting. Giving a man like Vlad what he wants wouldn't guarantee my father's freedom but only secure his death."

Prince pulled up his briefs and jeans, his wet hair clinging to his neck. "He has two daughters to worry about. Why would he put your lives at risk, knowing that time would only reveal your existence?"

She covered her eyes, pacing in a circle. "Oh God, Charming. I don't know what to do." Kat lowered her hands and looked at him guiltily. "What if he called? I'm down here rolling around in the dirt and—"

"Taken care of," he assured her. "My phone is in my pocket, and I can guarantee if anyone had contacted the house, my men would be down here faster than you could catch your breath."

"I can't just sit here. It's not in my nature."

The sound of water trickling from the ceiling above and splashing on the stony floor muted out small noises.

Kat wiped a rogue tear away before Prince saw it. She knew she needed to rest or she'd be useless, but during the quiet moments, her mind wouldn't stop thinking about Nadia. Patience was necessary in her line of work and had always been something that came naturally to her. But this was personal, something that made time her enemy. Her eyes were heavy-lidded and her body weak.

The room spun when Prince lifted her off her feet and carried her toward the stairs. His strength was unmatched, and she felt silly for feeling so protected in his embrace when she needed no protection.

"What are you doing?" she mumbled, resting her head on his shoulder.

He headed up the stairs, breathing a little heavier. "You try so hard to be strong, but sometimes you need to be weak."

"That makes about as much sense as eating soup with a fork."

"It's the only way someone can take care of you the way you deserve to be." Prince kicked open the door and moved quickly down the hall, ascending another flight of stairs. "I want you to let me take care of you. Give me one night to protect you and see that you're fed. Let me bathe you until you're clean and then put you to bed."

Kat chuckled quietly. "My bad habits are rubbing off on you, Charming. You rhymed." She curled against him, warming to his soft words and generous offer. "And then?"

"And then my wolf will guard you until dawn."

"What if someone tries to come in?"

He answered without hesitation. "Then he'll die."

She believed him. This wasn't about seduction; Prince was wooing her the way a Shifter pursued a mate. It was an honor to have a wolf guard your bed while you slept or bring you food from a hunt. It was an instinct and tradition among mated couples that dated back as far as anyone could remember.

When he entered his bedroom, he closed the door and leaned against it, still holding her in his arms. She felt at home when she looked into his mismatched eyes, deciding she couldn't pick a favorite between the two. They each were different, but both looked at her with the same affection.

"Charming?"

"Yes?"

"I'm probably going to cry a little bit, so I need you to let me do that without any judgment, or else you can leave the room. I know how men freeze up like a pipe in a snowstorm when women get emotional."

His words were nothing but a gentle breath. "I'm not going anywhere."

CHAPTER 11

P RINCE CHECKED ON KAT FOR the fifth time since shifting back to human form. Morning light crept up the balcony and made the bedroom look as if it were spun from gold. The night before had surpassed any he'd spent with a woman in all his lifetimes.

Kat let him bathe her and rub scented oils on her skin. She shared small talk with him while they ate a meal together—tomato-basil soup and fresh-baked bread. But her appetite wasn't what he'd grown accustomed to, and after finishing only half her meal, she wanted to lie down.

Sleep didn't come quickly, so he made her a glass of warm honey water with cinnamon. She protested at first, claiming it looked like puddle mud after a hard rain, but a sip was all it took to convince her otherwise.

In the secrecy of darkness, Kat had wept in his arms. Wept for what he imagined was the fear that she might never see her twin again. Prince offered no words of comfort because there *were* none. He knew the emptiness of losing a sibling, and sometimes the only remedy is to grieve. Once her tears subsided, she fell asleep in his arms. Kat had a peculiar habit of kicking all the covers off. It seemed that the only thing she wanted covering her body was him. He stayed that way for a while to make sure she felt his protection, because the power emitted from an alpha wolf was all-encompassing, like a blanket. After what seemed like an hour, he finally shifted. Prince remained aware for as long as he could stay awake, and when he chose to sleep, his wolf took over the duty of guarding his love.

His love. Not someone else's; not an abstract idea, but a woman he wanted at his side, in his bed, leading his pack, and sharing his meals. A woman he would kill for. A woman he barely knew and yet felt a timeless connection between them that he couldn't ignore. That was love, wasn't it?

Prince had acquired respect, power, and wealth over the years. He possessed more sway with the Councils and higher authority than most, and damn if he was going to sit idly by while Vlad ripped apart lives once again.

When Kat finally awoke, she was herself again. Strong, determined, resilient. Despite her claim of being shy, she approached the balcony nude and opened the doors, her body suffused in sunlight.

Prince was seated quietly in his chair, memorizing every line, the subtle way she would shift her hips, her dark hair blowing back from the gentle breeze, the sublime way sunlight touched the edges of her body until it glowed, and the regal way she turned around and settled her luminous eyes on him like a lover to a mate.

"I love watching you," he said offhandedly, resting his head against his closed fist.

Kat clutched her heart and quickly tiptoed to the bed, putting on her flannel shirt. "I didn't see you there. You kind of blend in with the furniture."

"I've been told that I'm wooden."

"I wouldn't go so far as to call you wooden, but you *are* a little antique," she said, a playful lilt in her voice. She left the top four buttons undone and gracefully approached him. "Just so you know, I don't do this with other guys."

"Make love?"

She sat on his lap and kissed his neck. "I meant crying, letting someone give me a bath and feed me, the oil massage… although that was one of the highlights."

"Incomparable to what we did in the basement?"

A smile touched her lips. "I like you, Charming."

"*Like?*"

He bristled at the word, because the way he felt for her was indescribable—a word he longed to hear from her lips.

Kat dodged his glare.

"I have many years ahead of me, Kat, and so do you. I'm going to guess you're already aware of this."

She nodded and rested her left arm over his shoulder. "My father told us we were purebloods. I believe that's why he was destroyed by our mother leaving, since it's so hard to find another like us. Not that he wanted more kids or anything, but I guess he thought old royalty should stay together."

"Did he love her?"

"Maybe it was a mating of convenience at first, but I think he fell in love with her. I just don't think she loved him back."

That made Prince's heart stop. He'd given her everything a male could in one night, but was that enough to make a woman give a man her heart?

"Anyhow," she went on, "I don't think she hated us. On one hand, I think she was selfish to leave her children, but on the other hand, we were better off with our father. We grew up in Russia under the protection of my father's pack. He wouldn't have wanted my mother dragging us around the country with her new mate like a band of gypsies. I just wish she would have at least visited us instead of cutting all ties."

"How long did you stay?"

She nestled against him, circling her finger against his bare chest. "Until we were about nine. Then Papa wanted to move to America. The pack was divided, but most of them came along. When we came of age, Nadia moved back to Russia. She got a job at a prestigious museum, but I think she really went back to find our mother. After ten years, she moved here but didn't want anything to do with living with a pack."

He was saddened by this story—that two girls were estranged from their mother most of their lives. "And your mother is still in Russia?"

She nodded. "How come you don't talk to me like you do with Nadia?"

He brushed her tangled hair away from her face so he could read her expression. "I'm not certain what you mean."

"On the rooftop, you were Mr. Chatty with her, but I always feel like I'm doing all the talking when we're together."

He squeezed her gently. "I spend too much time talking. It's refreshing to hear what you have to say. And besides, your sister's version of conversation is stilted and about superficial things. She's not as forthright as she perceives herself to be."

Kat flattened her hand on his bare chest. He liked the feel of her in his arms, the casualness of the way she showed her affection.

"You have to catch her in a good mood and she'll open up. Sometimes she's so concerned about what other people will think about her that she doesn't know how to talk to someone. I don't care about opinions. I say what's on my mind and you either like it or you don't. Maybe I'm too blunt and cuss too much…"

He pressed a soft kiss to her forehead and she lifted her chin, silently demanding one to her lips. He obliged, but only on the corner of her mouth. "It wasn't long ago I would have found a woman with your tongue crass and offensive."

She nibbled his bottom lip and purred, "How do you like my tongue now?"

"I'm not sure. Let me taste…"

When their kiss deepened, Prince stirred with arousal.

Kat abruptly pulled back and patted his chest. "Not now. I have too much on my mind."

"I had no intentions of the sort."

She wiggled her bottom, creating a delicious friction between them and causing Prince to throw back his head and suck in a sharp breath. Kat placed a kiss on his Adam's apple and then beneath his chin. "Could have fooled me. Get dressed. I want to tear this town inside out until I get my sister back."

"I'll bring you my laptop so you can review his files."

"Thanks," she said, easing off his lap. "I don't think he'll have anything in there that'll reveal his whereabouts, but I'm pretty sure there's enough incriminating evidence to turn over to the higher authority."

"He's *already* deemed an outlaw. What purpose would that serve?" Prince rose to his feet and frowned.

Kat put her hands on her hips and stuck out her leg. "If he's slave trading, then he's got juicy info in those files. Not only will it lead to more arrests and putting those criminals where they belong, but it might lead to finding and freeing some of the victims. Imagine all the people out there who think the world has forgotten about them, and they've given up all hope. It's good to know at the end of day that I helped someone, but I don't always get that feeling with this job. They don't usually offer me cases to bust up rings since I don't have a partner. Plus, let's face it," she said, turning on her heel, "the higher authority is predominantly male, and most of them still believe a woman can't do a man's job."

"Men have been fools since the beginning of time."

"I want that on a T-shirt." Kat stepped into a clean pair of underwear and jeans he'd left for her, giving him an appraising glance. "You should dress like that more often."

He looked down at his silk pajama bottoms.

"I like the whole sexy long-hair thing you've got going on. And the bare-chested pajama ensemble is a good look on you. Especially barefoot."

He glanced down at her, closing his brown eye and squinting with the other. "Are you mocking me?"

His question was answered almost immediately when she smoothed her hands across his chest and made him shiver. Her lips grazed over his nipple, tongue circling around the hardened tip.

"I'm serious. It's casual and I like it," she said. "I'd really like to see this behind me on a sofa while we're watching TV, so make that happen. Eating Chinese food and cuddling can be just as sexy as exotic oils and our naked bodies pressed together. Well… not quite the same, but you'll see what I mean."

He arched his brow. "Perhaps you can plan our next date while I retrieve the laptop for your research."

"Swell. I hope you have a Cracker Barrel around here, because not only do I love their chicken and dumplings, but I could *live* in their gift shop. Buy me some peanut brittle and I'll be your girl."

He circled his arms about her waist. "I would also like to know what you sleep in."

"First of all, I don't have my usual clothes with me. Secondly, I don't go all the way on the first date."

A smile hovered on his lips. "And what would you call last night?"

Her soft lips pressed against his, sable eyes looking up at him. "Definitely not a date."

"Are you hungry?"

"You wouldn't happen to have any french toast, would you?"

Prince smirked and opened the door. "I think I can make that happen. How does bacon on the side sound?"

Kat licked her lip seductively. "Yummy."

⊸∘⋐⋑∘⊶

Kat reviewed the data on the flash drive three times, hoping some scrap of information would let her uncover where Vlad was keeping Nadia and her father. Yet the only thing she found was one disgusting transaction after another.

She'd eaten two helpings of french toast and six pieces of bacon. The man brought her maple bacon. Kat was pretty sure if she was ever on death row, her last meal would probably be ten pounds of maple bacon. She had a sneaking suspicion that Prince hadn't cooked it, but his shortcomings were forgiven the moment he asked if it was to her satisfaction. The rich timbre of his voice made her melt like chocolate over a fire, as did the shoulder rub.

And when he fed her a piece of bacon.

An hour later, Prince called Russell into the room for an update.

Russell hiccupped, finishing off a piece of bacon. "Vlad's house was empty, the motor gone, and the stove still warm by the time we'd gotten there last night." Russell pulled Prince toward the door behind her and attempted to lower his voice. Kat hung on his every word while she pretended to work, giving him the respect of privacy with his packmate.

"A basement?" Prince asked in disbelief. "I didn't see a basement when I was there."

"Aye. Someone's been living down there a long time. It was

hidden and soundproofed behind a faux bookshelf. There were bits of stale bread and hair on the floor... and fresh blood."

Kat froze as they continued their conversation. While they were behind her, she was skilled at visualizing positions and body movements based on sounds. When she heard a rustle of fabric as someone turned, she continued scribbling nonsense on paper.

"What kind of hair?" Prince continued.

"A few different kinds, actually. Traces of wolf hair all over, but they also found a long strand."

"Blond?"

"Aye. Unless he's traversing in the woods with a Shifter on a leash, my guess is he's not gone too far. We're scanning motels for recent check-ins, but that takes a wee bit of time."

"Vlad will scheme something before he makes contact. We need to locate him fast."

Kat listened to Russell scratching the whiskers on his face. "That's a problem. One I suppose you can't help unless we find his rabbit hole."

"Did you get any sleep?"

Kat peered over her shoulder at Russell as he rubbed his face, eyes swollen with exhaustion. "No, there's no sense in it now, sire. We got a few false leads from the bulletin; a stiff reward always does that. Not to worry. His motor will be easy to spot with the front-end damage. We have men ready to move."

"My men?"

"Some of them, aye. The rest owe me a favor... or a pint."

The door closed and strong hands cupped her shoulders. Prince placed a quick kiss on her temple and then lightly rested his chin on top of her head. "What are we looking at?"

She reached up and held his hands. "A whole lotta nothing. At least, not where my family's concerned. I did find a list of buyers he's worked with, so I'm e-mailing it to my contact in the higher authority. I left all my equipment behind to chase Vlad, so thanks for lending me your laptop."

"All that is mine is yours."

He straightened and circled around her, sitting on the edge of his desk. Prince still hadn't gotten dressed, and as far as Kat was concerned, he could waltz around in his black pajama bottoms forever.

"Is this how you spoil all your women?" She twisted her chair back and forth in short semicircles.

"If this is your indirect way of asking me about my past, I'll readily admit I've never been mated."

"Never crossed your mind in seven hundred years of fornication?"

He blinked rapidly and then averted his eyes. "It crosses my mind frequently, but I was raised with expectations of continuing my bloodline with royalty. There are few purebloods who survived the great wars. Only once had I considered settling for less, although there were circumstances in that situation that made her suitable."

Kat pursed her lips and then crossed her legs. "*Suitable*," she said, letting the unpleasant word play on her tongue.

"Mating with another pureblood is an obligation I have to my ancestors, one that will allow a dying line to continue. Tell me what you're thinking?"

Kat was never one to censor her thoughts. "I'm just thinking how convenient it is for you that I came along. What if I wasn't from royal blood and was just like any other woman?"

"I cannot say what I would do in hypothetical situations," he replied. "But I can assure you it's not your bloodline that intrigues me. You also forget that it's not as if I don't have a choice."

Her brow arched. "*Nadia?* You might want to extract your foot from your mouth, because implying I should be grateful that you chose me over my twin sister doesn't win you any brownie points. Especially if you think I'm easier to claim, because despite Nadia's fussy standards, I'm the one who's not easily swayed by a Packmaster's power and money."

Prince stepped in front of her and leaned down, gripping the armrests of her leather chair. "*You* are the obvious choice. When I look at her, the more I see your differences, not your similarities. What you didn't allow me to say was that I have a lot to offer a woman, and that gives me options. Perhaps Nadia would be the preferred choice of those I'm surrounded by, but I also have the choice to reject."

Kat snorted. "You don't intimidate me, Charming." She poked his bare chest with her finger and pushed him back. "Just remember that the choice isn't just yours, and I'm not a woman easily wooed by—"

"Exotic oils and primal sex?"

"I was going to say yummy soup and a comfy bed, but that too." She twisted her hair back and sighed, distracted once again by thoughts of Vlad.

Prince leaned back against the desk, folding his arms. "Is this what a day in your life is like?"

She lifted her shoulder in a shrug.

He nodded, a look of admiration shining in his eyes. Alpha men were attracted to strong women, regardless if those women were alphas or not. Kat had forgotten what it was like to have a man look at her that way—with affection and admiration. She hadn't felt that kind of acceptance since her father's disappearance.

She was a little put off by his cocky attitude, behaving as if she was an easy catch. Maybe she needed to make the chase a little harder so she didn't look like the fish that jumped into the fisherman's boat. Then again, this wasn't the time to be selfishly planning her future; Nadia needed her.

"Why don't you have tattoos like the other Packmasters?" she asked.

Most had identifying tattoos of some kind. In a busy town full of Shifters, you might not know all the Packmasters personally, but you'd recognize their markings from hearing about them.

He waved his hand. "These young pups don't understand the significance of inking their bodies. I don't require a mark to establish my power. And aside from that, those who do not know me will have heard about my strange eye color."

"Your taste in furniture is stranger than your eye color." She tugged the collar of her shirt, revealing her bare shoulder. "I've been thinking about getting a tribal marking on my arm. What do you think?"

His lips thinned. "I think you say things to get a rise out of me."

"I didn't say much when I got a rise out of you last night."

He turned away, and she admired the shape of his back and how it angled down from his broad shoulders. She remembered what it felt like to run her fingers over those lines, the feel of his muscles rippling as he claimed her.

"I'm going to enjoy pursuing you immensely," he said almost to himself.

The chair squeaked when Kat stood up. She circled her right arm about his waist as they strolled toward the open balcony doors. "You're old enough to be my father."

He caught her left wrist and, in a quick motion, swung her in front of him. "I age remarkably well."

"Tell me about the view from the pyramids," she teased, smiling up at him.

"Someday you will be as old as I am, brave wolf."

She backed up a step, a cool breeze at her back. "Yes, but I'll have less interesting things to discuss in comparison to all your stories. You can entertain guests with the invention of electricity or the discovery of America. I'll get to enlighten them on fast food, television, and bacon ice cream."

His nose wrinkled.

Kat tapped it with her finger. "Never had bacon in your ice cream? Bucket list!" She moved away in search of her shoes.

"I'm not familiar with that phrase."

"It's a list of things you want to do before you die."

"Hmm," he said, eyes brimming with curiosity. "Then why call it a bucket?"

"As in kicking the bucket. Boy, you really need to get out more. People say TV kills your brain cells, but it also dials you in to the twenty-first century." Kat peered underneath the bed and found her shoes, quickly shoving her feet into them without socks. "I need to get my boots out of my car. I'd rather get blisters than trip all over these laces. By the way, thanks for doing my laundry, but you didn't have to give me all that," she said, motioning toward a pile of clothes on a table between the bed and long mirror in the corner.

It wasn't uncommon for her to wear the same clothes for days in a row because of her job. The sniff test worked fine, and most people she associated with in bars couldn't smell anything except the stench of cigarettes or their own cologne, so having someone wash her clothes and buy her new ones seemed excessive.

But thoughtful.

An urgent knock sounded at the door. Prince rushed to answer, his hair still loose and unkempt.

Russell lowered a pear from his mouth and chewed twice before speaking. "Perhaps you should get dressed," he suggested with a flash of humor in his eyes. "You have a visitor downstairs, and I don't think you'll impress him with your fancy trousers."

CHAPTER 12

P RINCE LED RENO COLE, AUSTIN'S second-in-command, into a private room and closed the door. "Can I offer you a drink?"

"How 'bout a cold one?" Reno rubbed his jaw, his cheeks and nose red from riding his motorcycle in the sun without a helmet.

Prince eyed his liquor cabinet full of expensive alcohol. He didn't stock beer because most guests would find it insulting for a Packmaster of his caliber to serve them cheap alcohol.

Reno patted his shoulder and chuckled. "Some of that whiskey's fine."

The amber liquid splashed in a crystal glass, and he swirled it before handing it to Reno.

The Weston pack lived in the territory, and Prince held a strong alliance with the newly formed pack. A tight bond existed within their family that made them strong and dependable allies despite the modest size of their pack.

"Everything is going well?" Prince inquired, taking a seat in the chair across from Reno.

"Dandy," Reno replied, sipping on his stiff drink.

Prince often used this quaint, less formal room for men who liked a good cigar and a glass of brandy. Reno wouldn't be impressed with his gold room, and it might have made him uncomfortable. Prince had never reached out to another pack for assistance, so he wanted this meeting to go smoothly.

"I've got to admit, you're the last man I expected to call me with a job. Respectfully, of course," Reno said, lifting his glass.

"Were you able to uncover any information on Vladimir Romanov?"

Reno frowned and widened his legs, tapping his boot heel on the floor. He set down his glass on the table to his left and began spinning a small globe that sat atop it. "Nothing came up on my radar showing any recent trades—at least not using that name."

"He's used an alias before, and that could be a problem." Prince traced his finger along his brow. "I don't think he's here for business. I believe this is a holding station of some kind—perhaps where he keeps his captives while locating a buyer. He maintains a home outside city limits, one with a hidden basement."

Reno's lips peeled back and his gaze drifted away. "Men like that are the reason why I love my fucking job. I can't help you if he's not trading around here; he might as well be a ghost." After another sip of whiskey, Reno's gravelly voice smoothed out. "How's that pretty blonde doing—the one you offered a ride to? I couldn't help but notice you noticing her," he said with a chuckle. "She would have been a handful for Denver, but I get the feeling a woman like that would be right up your alley."

"The man you're looking for took her."

With lightning speed, Reno shot up to his feet and clenched his fists. The tension was palpable.

A knot twisted in Prince's stomach, but he maintained composure. "I'm doing everything in my power to find her, and I hope you'll continue to offer your assistance."

Reno's voice became low and dangerous. "I ain't gonna sugarcoat it for you. If I find him, I'm going to put him in the ground."

Prince admired the wolf before him. Reno didn't know Nadia, but a noble man didn't need a personal connection to take a stand for what was right.

"No need," Prince said with a dismissive wave of his hand. "I'll be doing the honors myself."

"I don't blame you. If someone took *my* woman—"

The doorknob jiggled, and both men turned to look.

"A person could get lost in this place," Kat said, out of breath, inviting herself in with a dramatic swing in her step. "It's like a labyrinth. Hey, did you ever see that movie? I always wanted to be Sarah, but what was the deal with Jareth? A formidable goblin king and the best he can do is white spandex and puffy shirts? *Fear me, love me, do as I say?*" She laughed. "If any man ever said that to me, I'd stuff him in a mailbox and return to sender. But that's just my opinion."

Prince rose to his feet, his eyes drinking in the way she glided across the room in his direction.

Reno's expression altered as he stared at Kat's familiar features and then glared at Prince. "Are you messing with me?"

Prince curved his arm around Kat when she stood beside him, then began with the introductions. "This is my lover, Katarina Kozlov." He refrained from smiling when he felt her hand claw at his back, apparently shocked by his open declaration. Or more precisely, his claim.

Reno folded his arms and gave Kat a hard look.

"Kat, this is Reno Cole. He's the private investigator I was telling you about."

An awkward silence hung in the room, and Prince didn't like the way Reno was staring at her.

"You look like the blonde," Reno said.

Kat stepped away from Prince and lifted her chin, hands on her hips. "She's my twin."

He studied her a moment longer and then smiled. "Yeah, I'm a little familiar with the twin situation. You sure as hell don't dress alike."

"I'm the one with style," she quipped.

When Reno's eyes widened at Kat, Prince followed the direction of his gaze.

"Kat!" Prince gripped the end of her shirt and tugged it back down.

"That's a hell of a custom job," Reno said under his breath.

Prince knew she was just showing off the holster for her dagger, but jealousy bloomed unexpectedly.

Kat touched her shirt. "It's a tight fit with expandable elastic— quality material, not the cheap stuff. So when I shift, it stays securely on my wolf and I never have to worry about losing a weapon."

"Nice. Think your guy can make me one for my gun?"

"Maybe." A wistful look crossed her expression. "I'm thinking about settling down here in Austin and getting into your line of work. Just an idea I'm tossing around since working for the higher authority can be demanding."

Reno's eyes flashed at Prince. "She's a bounty hunter?"

Prince realized he was going to be hearing that question a lot, and his first instinct was to lift his chin and maintain eye contact. He was proud of his chosen female.

A slow chuckle rose in Reno and he patted Prince on the shoulder. "You've got bigger balls than I gave you credit for. Hope you're up for the task. Men like us aren't easy to live with."

Kat chortled. "What gave my gender away—my thick bed of chest hair?"

A bloom of red touched Reno's face, and he rubbed his clean-shaven jaw. "I meant women too. Men *and* women. Uh… Just an expression."

Kat's smile waned. "Are you here to help find my sister?"

"I hired Reno to see if Vlad has any contacts in the area," Prince said, clasping his hands together. "My intent was to uncover any associates who might have taken him in and given him refuge."

She looked at him with hope glittering in her eyes. "And?"

"He's not trading in Austin, not unless he's working under an alias we don't know about."

Kat waved her arms, exasperated. "Now what? I looked through all the files and couldn't find a connection here. Transaction dates and amounts, but no second home and definitely no alias that I could find. Vlad has my sister, and time is of the fucking essence! Why did he just get up in the middle of a bar and drive all the way down to Austin so he could hang out in a shack in the woods? It doesn't make any sense!"

Prince lowered his head but kept his eyes on her. "We think he's been holding Alex prisoner. There was wolf hair and fresh blood in the basement, and not from Nadia's wolf. I'm assuming since you're twins, her wolf is black, like yours. He probably drives down every so often to feed him. A Shifter can go a long time without food or water, so maybe Vlad left him a few supplies. I thought you would have guessed this?"

Kat shielded her face with one hand, only her mouth visible. "I did. I just needed to hear someone say it out loud to confirm I'm not crazy—that my father's still alive. That I haven't been holding out hope all these years in vain."

Reno cleared his throat and flashed Prince a look, the kind a man gives when he sees a woman in distress. "Well, I'm not completely useless. We don't have any associates, but I got the names of two local men known to run with him. Not business partners that I can tell, probably just lackeys. It's the best lead we've got."

Kat discreetly wiped her wet lashes. "And where are his buddies?"

"My guy only knows them by first name, but he gave me a good description. He's seen them hanging around. I got a feeling Vlad pays them to move the Shifters he's selling. If he's got your sister and anyone else, he'll need help." Reno stroked his bottom lip with his thumb. "We need to move fast since he might be using their vehicles to transport them out of the city. I don't think he'll make a move in the daytime, but I'll call you the second I get word, so keep your phone on," he said, turning his attention to Prince.

Kat reached under her shirt, and Prince smirked when he heard the sound of Velcro. She pulled out a miniature pen. "Give me your arm," she said to Reno.

He stuck out his arm with a bemused expression.

"This is my number, just in case Prince's battery dies or a moose eats it. Memorize it and then wipe it off. I don't like my number floating around on paper... or flesh."

"You got it."

———— ⊸∘⟨⟩∘⊸ ————

Kat tried to keep herself occupied, but all she could think about was putting a dagger into Vlad's eye. Prince led her to the media room, but it was awkward sitting amidst a strange pack, especially after Prince introduced her as his lover. That had roused a few curious glances.

Lover was such an old-fashioned term—something only Frenchmen used in the movies. Then again, Prince was Old World European, so to him the word held a significant meaning. She didn't argue since she couldn't come up with an acceptable word herself. They weren't mated, and calling a seven-hundred-year-old alpha her boyfriend seemed unquestionably inappropriate.

Kat headed down to the basement, hoping a shift would settle her nerves and kill some time. But once there, her wolf didn't want out. So she sat down on a flat rock, pulled up her knees, and rested her chin on top of her folded arms.

Thoughts flitted through her mind. Did Vlad know Nadia was her twin sister, or was he just using her to barter with? Vlad must have realized Prince was a powerful Packmaster who would turn this city upside down to find her, so revenge didn't seem likely. Kat was certain Vlad wanted something from her father, and he assumed she had it in her possession. But what?

She sat back and circled her fingers across the strap that went over her left shoulder. Would Vlad accept money in exchange for her sister? That left her with hope, but if he had her father, he wasn't going to let go as easily. Just thinking about her father in captivity, starving to death, made her want to break something. Worse, she'd been in the very house Vlad might have been holding her father in. He could have been right beneath her feet the whole time she was messing around on the stupid computer!

"Ouch!" Kat snapped her hand back and looked at the tip of her finger, rubbing away the sting. It felt similar to static shock, and she looked at the strap to make sure it wasn't damaged.

After rubbing her finger over the same spot a few times, she didn't feel anything unusual. Might have been a splinter stuck in the weave. Yet this felt different.

"I've been looking for you," Prince said from across the room. He stalked over the grass and put one foot on the rock where she sat. "What are you doing?"

Kat stripped off her shirt.

"So soon?"

She cut him a sharp glare. "Something's wrong."

"That bra looks becoming on you," he said with smooth satisfaction, looking more handsome than he had a right to. "I'm just disappointed it was Reno who got the first glimpse."

Kat preferred to be braless because her wolf couldn't slip out of a bra during the shift when she was wearing the harness. That meant her wolf would be prancing around in a bra, which had happened once in a bar down in El Paso.

She took off the holster and ran the strap between her fingers, turning it over. It was thickly padded on the side that lay against her body, and there were several pouches sewn across the outside.

"My father was the one who customized this for me. He told me to always wear it, and he knows I'm a sentimental person."

"He did nice work," Prince said, kneeling down and giving it a closer inspection.

"Yeah, it's actually comfy." Kat pulled out the dagger and ran the pointy tip beneath one of the pouches.

"What are you doing, Kat?"

Once she made the cut wide enough, she set down the blade and pushed her pinky finger inside. Within the space was something cool to the touch, so she hooked her finger until she got a grip on it.

Kat slid out a ring and held it in the palm of her hand.

Prince took it between two fingers and examined the ruby stone. "This... this belongs to Vlad. His companions used to joke that someone would cut his throat for the stone, so he often wore it with the stone facing down."

Kat looked closely at her harness where a pocket had been made to conceal the ring. Her father was clever to have hidden the piece so it wouldn't be in his possession.

"What was my father doing with Vlad's ring?"

Prince furrowed his dark brows, his hair neatly pulled back, much to her dismay. "I think it's infused with magic. In Russia, the Mageri—who uphold the laws for his kind—didn't exist. Creators held more power and chose human warriors to put their first spark into—strong men who would not only remain loyal to them in order to learn the Mage ways, but who would also protect them as an army of men would a king. But the average Mage is not a Creator, and once granted independence, they go off to wreak whatever havoc they desire."

"They're not all bad," Kat added. "They were smart to form the Mageri early on because it set the tone for the other Breeds to establish some kind of order. Sorry, didn't mean to interrupt."

"Men like Vlad created their own law, aligning with others and mirroring the military organizations they saw in the human world. They preyed on weak men and those who didn't have protection. So you can imagine the number of enemies they made. Certain metals and stones can hold Mage energy, and in those times, they considered these trinkets invaluable."

"But why a ring instead of a dagger?"

"What could be more innocuous?" He turned the gold band between his fingers, a glint of light reflecting off the edge. "They didn't have the communication devices we do now to form a black market, so it wasn't easy to obtain stunners and other weapons infused with magic. In those times, a select few had the rare talent to lock large amounts of energy into metal. A Mage could pull from it for a boost of strength, but I've heard stories of some containing dark magic. Most were probably tall tales meant to strike fear about what a Mage could do, but I suspect there was a sliver of truth to some of it."

"Like what?"

"Knowing what I know now about their gifts, the possibilities of what they can infuse in metals are infinite. What happened that made you notice it?"

She shook her head, trying to remember. "I was just sitting here being pissed off at Vlad. I must have been rubbing my finger along the edge."

"Did it move?"

She took the ring from him and let the oversized piece swallow her index finger. "No, it felt like a tiny electric shock. Do you think it reacted to my anger?"

"We could test it. Get angry."

Kat laughed. "Easier said than done."

He leaned forward with a detached expression, one that made

her stomach flutter, but not in a good way. "Think about me taking your sister to bed."

"Ouch!" Kat flicked her wrist and the ring sailed into the grass.

"Cursed with Mage power," he whispered, picking it up again.

She rubbed her finger and frowned. "I've been angry lots of times while wearing the holster; why didn't it shock me before?"

"The thick padding on the inside would have protected you from its power. Alex must have inserted a protective layer of special material between your skin and the ring to create a barrier, and I'm assuming you don't spend much time touching the outer layer. When the gold encircles the finger—like just now—you can access its full power."

Kat was feeling dizzy from all this Mage talk. "Your old magic confuses me. What would be the benefit of having a ring that shocks a person when they're mad?"

"For you it might be a shock, but for a Mage, it's a source of energy that strengthens their abilities. I don't know; I'm only guessing. Mage magic has always confounded me. If this is what Vlad is searching for, then it must be far more powerful than we can sense."

"Maybe it's just sentimental and his Mage daddy gave it to him."

Prince closed his hand into a tight fist. "If that's true, then this trinket will be what gives us an advantage. Now that we have what he wants, we can bargain."

She tried to take it, but Prince moved his arm out of reach and she scowled. "You can't just *give* it to him! In the real world, each side is conspiring how to get what they want without giving up what they have. That's what scares me, Charming. He's got my father *and* sister. If I give him this ring, he's not going to set them free. We have to find him before he flees the city."

Prince began to slowly unbutton his shirt, stripping out of it and folding it on the grass with the ring on top.

An ancient heat coursed through her veins; her desire for him was insatiable. "What are you up to, Charming?"

"Don't take off the bra," he said, slowly unbuttoning her jeans. "Your temper makes me want to feel that fire against me. We need something to do while we're waiting, and I have an excellent suggestion for how to cool you down."

Kat threw back her head, his breath skating across her hips and stomach, unraveling her from inside out. "I always did like a man with a plan."

CHAPTER 13

A FTER HOURS OF LOVEMAKING, PRINCE had eagerly wrapped his arms around Kat and placed kisses on her forehead, cheeks, and mouth. This time there had been more tenderness between them, and it enriched their intimacy that much more. While she showered upstairs, he checked with Russell for a status update. There had been no new findings, which made him uneasy as he knew Kat was growing impatient and might slip out to hunt down Vlad by herself.

Uncertain of where the day might take him, he changed into a pair of black pants and a dark grey shirt. Prince's wardrobe wasn't just suits, but also long-sleeve cotton shirts and casual dress shirts. He preferred button-ups or a cotton shirt beneath a suit jacket. Today's choice wasn't about presentation; he needed to choose clothing that would be practical for chasing and killing an outlaw.

"Make sure you put a good pair of running shoes on your Christmas wish list," Kat said, glancing down at his leather shoes. She reached up and removed the white towel from her head, shaking out long strands of wet hair. "Now I don't feel like an exhumed body. I think next time we should use a bed… like normal people."

Prince stirred with amusement because there was no question, despite her little quips, that Kat liked the wildness of their lovemaking. He watched her open the balcony doors and lean over the railing, sunlight and wind drying her beautiful waves of black hair. A moment later, she sneezed and headed back inside.

"Something's floating around in the air."

"Yes, it certainly is," he mused, watching how she took command of any room she was in. Her absence made Prince consider how vacant his life had been without her. Not just a woman *like* her, but Kat.

Water soaked through her grey shirt, and she looked between them with a melancholy grin. "We match." Her smile withered as she sat on his lap, resting her head against his chest. "Do you think we'll still like each other when this is all over?"

Prince kissed the top of her head. "I think there's a possibility."

"We collided in a twist of fate, and maybe the only thing holding us together is your personal interest in finding my father."

He rested his chin on her head and sighed, his voice falling to a soft murmur. "My personal interest is you."

"Don't get me wrong. I like you, Charming. It's just that I deal with chaos on a daily basis, and sometimes coming off that adrenaline rush is a cold splash of reality."

"There you go again with that word I loathe."

"What word?"

Prince tried not to show his distaste for it in his tone. "Like."

Her giggle tickled his chest. "I don't know why you have such an aversion to a word that means I feel something positive for you. Don't you think it would be a little premature for me to say I love you when we only just met?"

"Just met, just met," he grumbled. "Young wolves play by such different rules, so unwilling to follow their instincts and their hearts. I suppose a man can't court you unless you know his favorite color or ice cream flavor?"

She sat up, batting away a wet strand of hair that had slipped in front of her face. Her brown eyes were invasive, traveling all the way down to the dark corners of his soul. "First of all, I don't think you're an expert in the love department any more than I am. There's nothing wrong with getting to know someone before making a life-changing decision."

"Will my favorite song tell you what kind of man I am in a way that making love to you won't? Will my favorite dessert reveal more about my character than laying down my life for you?"

She worried her bottom lip and lifted her brows. "I see your point, but you'll have to play along if you're interested in pursuing me. I've never had a man chase me so hard, and it scares me. How do I know I love you if I've never loved a man?"

His heart warmed, and he brushed his fingers down her cheek. "You know it's love when you cannot live without a person, the way you've spent years pursuing your father. The way you cannot sleep until you know your sister's safe. Love is when the thought of losing that very thing is so unbearable that you find it difficult to breathe."

"And how would you know something like that?" she asked, tilting her head.

His hand slid down and rested over her heart. "Because that's how I feel about you, Katarina. I'm seasoned enough to know the difference between infatuation and something real. My wolf thirsts for the blood of any man who would harm you, and those are more than words but a promise. Even speaking of it now..." He lifted her hand to his jugular so she could feel his pulse quickening.

Kat's eyes searched his, her hand cupping his neck. "I don't know if I want someone loving me that hard. I tend to disappoint people. Think about it, Charming. A big-shot Packmaster mated with a bounty hunter doesn't look so shiny on a piece of paper. The local Council would flip their lids."

Amusement danced in his eyes and he patted her leg. "I love the way you talk. I'm going to enjoy the conversation I plan to have with Alex about you."

"*That* should be interesting. I don't know if my father would like his best friend dating his daughter. You should see how he scared off the last guy who thought he was good enough to court a Packmaster's daughter."

"Did he get out a crossbow?"

A small line appeared between her eyebrows when she frowned. "How did you know that?"

"I know your father, and he's not an ambivalent man. He's a good judge of character."

The door swung open and hit the wall. "Sire!"

Prince flew out of his chair, Kat spinning behind him. "What have I told you about coming in unannounced?"

Russell's face bloomed red—a mixture of anger and

embarrassment as he looked between the two. He lowered his eyes respectfully and stepped back.

"Come in," Prince said, waving his hand. "What's changed?"

Russell strode forward, rubbing his temples. "Someone spotted his motor and called it in. I sent Greta to stay on his arse."

"Good choice," Prince said as they moved out of the room and down the hall, his long strides forcing Kat to jog to keep up with him. "I want everyone to return home and stay where they are. I won't be here to command the pack, so I trust you'll keep an eye on things while I'm away."

Russell tried to block Prince and ended up walking backward. "Hold up there, sire. It's a wee bit dangerous for a Packmaster." He grimaced. "I don't mean it like that," he said, smacking himself in the forehead. "Our duty is to protect our leader and follow orders. You're the general, and without the general, there's no army."

Kat finally caught up and stepped between them. "What is *that* supposed to mean?" she snapped. "It doesn't sound like you have any confidence that your Packmaster can hold his own."

"Wait a minute…" Russell held out both hands, dodging the accusation. "I don't think our Packmaster needs advice from a poke."

The air stilled when Kat stopped in her tracks. "What did you just call me? For your information, I'm *not* just a good fuck."

Russell's eyes quickly flashed to Prince, his cheeks mottled with scarlet. "I'll just be goin' now," he said, rushing out of sight.

Prince led her forward, uncertain whether to laugh or chase after Russell with a baseball bat. "I'll reprimand him later for that. You know, a lady shouldn't use foul language."

Kat hooked her arm in his. "I'm hardly a lady, but I sure like the way you talk, Charming."

Kat insisted on taking separate cars, arguing it was protocol in her line of work. He sensed she just needed to be behind a steering wheel, so she took her car and followed behind him.

Prince kept the ring in his possession since Kat had expressed concern about Vlad searching her. His black pants had several pockets with a flap, so Prince concealed it in one of the compartments on his right pant leg.

Going alone on a mission without his pack gave him a renewed sense of purpose. His father had discouraged him from forming a pack at a young age, instead teaching him how to build alliances. When Prince became a man, he remained within his father's pack, watching and learning. Sometimes when action was called for, Prince was the man to do the dirty work—a job his father said would test him as a man. This hunt brought back memories of an earlier time when he had fewer responsibilities and more freedom.

It brought out the hunter in him.

When his phone rang, he put it on speaker. "Greta, what's going on?"

"He's on the move."

"Stay close, and don't let him out of your sight."

"The sun's going down, but that's not the only thing going down. There are two cars. The second one is a dark blue sedan with a wolf decal on the back windshield. You can't miss it. If they split up, who do you want me to follow?"

Prince glanced in his rearview mirror at Kat. "Did you get a look at them?"

"I couldn't risk getting too close when they pulled out, but there's only one man in each car from what I can see."

"What about the location?"

"A guy named Reno showed up and stayed behind to check out the property. He said he's with the Weston pack and you hired him. He wanted me to relay the message."

The light turned green and Prince accelerated. "Good. Tell him to call me if he finds anything. If you don't have his number—"

She laughed. "I got it. He must have been military or something because he was barking out orders like Patton. He thought there might be captives inside, and that's when we split up."

"Which direction are you heading?"

The line went silent for a moment, followed by, "I lost them! I lost them!"

"What direction?" he shouted.

"North. North from the primary location. I got boxed in at a light and then they suddenly hit the gas and split up."

Prince had to make a decision. "Circle the area and keep an eye out in case they return to the house. You've done your job."

After hanging up, Prince headed north. It was the only direction Vlad would sensibly travel if he wanted to get out of the state; leaving the city wouldn't place him far enough out of Prince's reach.

His phone rang again, and this time it was Kat.

"What's going on?" she asked in a cool voice.

"What makes you think—"

"Because you missed the green light by five seconds?"

"My tracker lost him."

Through his mirror he watched her hitting the steering wheel, and colorful profanities filled the silence of his car. Prince didn't like how late it was getting—it would only make it harder to track Vlad. Darkness was descending as the streetlights twinkled with new light, and bats circled erratically in the dimming sky.

"Hang up so you don't miss his call," she finally said. "If he suspects for a minute that we're following him, he won't leave the city. Do we still have checkpoints set up on the main arteries?"

"Yes. Unless he knows the back roads, he won't get past the blockades."

"Charming?"

His eyes flicked up in the rearview mirror, but because of the headlights, all he could make out was the outline of her head. "Yes?"

"I don't know. I suddenly felt like I needed to tell you something, but I'm not sure what. Promise me you won't let him get away."

"You have my word."

"Stay safe."

Ten minutes later, the city was immersed in a shroud of darkness. Prince admired the beauty of lights that illuminated the streets. Few remembered a time as he did where only torches lit the way on a moonless night.

When his phone rang, he quickly answered. "Yes?"

"Well, if it isn't Prince himself. *Prince*. A man should have a full name. You are no better than the rest of us that you should only have one."

"I'm older than you, Vlad."

"Ah, but I'm a Mage and I'll outlive you."

We'll see about that, Prince thought, pulling over to the side of the road in front of a gas station.

"I feel like a conversation is in order," Vlad continued. "Bring the woman but no one else."

"Where?"

"You know the old bridge with the arch? Be here in five minutes."

Prince went from zero to sixty in four seconds. Tires screeched when Kat peeled out behind him, trying to keep up. The traffic thinned out, and it looked like a hill of rock had been sliced in half to accommodate the road. When they crossed onto Pennybacker Bridge, he saw Vlad standing behind his car with the hazard lights on.

"Vlad, you bastard. What are you up to?" he whispered.

He eased his car off to the right and Kat pulled up behind him, almost smashing into his bumper before hitting the brakes. He got out and approached Vlad, scanning his surroundings in search of anyone who might be lurking in the shadows.

Vlad sat against the front end of his car, arms folded and a flicker of madness in his eyes. If not for his modern clothes, he looked unchanged from the time Prince had known him centuries ago. Except cleaner.

Vlad's sardonic smile faltered when Kat rushed toward him in quick steps.

When she passed Prince, he gripped her arm and held her back.

"The fearless ones always die first," Vlad said gruffly. "You know, I much prefer you with blond hair."

"Where's my sister!"

His brows rose, revealing several long lines in his forehead. "Sister… or father? Once I threw her in with Alexei, he gave up her identity in a fit of rage. I didn't see the resemblance," Vlad said, a sonorous laugh escaping.

Prince spoke through clenched teeth. "Why did you summon us?"

"Yes, we are too old to play childish games."

"And yet you keep playing them," Kat snarled.

When Vlad cut his sharp eyes at her, Prince pulled her protectively to him.

"You see me as a depraved man, but you do not see the fault in those around you. Your father took something of mine I entrusted to him. He is nothing but a thief."

That made Prince rock with laughter. "And why should I believe that? You would entrust *nothing* to a man you imprisoned."

Vlad narrowed his eyes at a passing car. "Is that so? During the Breed exodus from Russia, his wolf was assigned to escort one of our generals out safely. We were ordered to stay behind and exterminate the prisoners. Alexei was supposed to return to the camp and meet his fate with his brethren, but I had promised him freedom if he would deliver something of mine to a trusted companion across the border. I made a special pouch for his wolf to keep it hidden beneath his fur, but instead of placing this item into safe hands, he put it in his pocket and escaped. Paid off the general with money he'd kept hidden from me."

Kat wriggled free from Prince's grasp. She took one step forward, and the wind lifted the long locks of her dark hair. "Good for him. A wrongfully imprisoned man outwitted you by patiently planning his escape. My father is a hunter and a fisherman, so he's a patient man by nature. I can't believe that after all these years you're still holding a grudge. Look at what century we're in," she exclaimed, holding out her arms. "It's time to let go of the past and get over your fucking ring."

Vlad pushed off the car and approached them, stopping short and cocking his head to the side. "Who said it was a ring?"

CHAPTER 14

A STAGGERING FACT ABOUT HUMANS IS how they ignore anything perceived as an inconvenience or a threat. It was something Kat couldn't relate to in the Breed world. The occasional car would drive past them on the bridge, not even bothering to slow down. It seemed like the shorter someone's lifespan was, the more they protected it, despite the cost to others.

So there they stood, on the side of a bridge at night for all the world to see, and yet no one was looking.

Vlad inched forward, his eyes ripe with malice. "Have you suddenly gone mute? What makes you think it was a *ring* I gave to your father?"

"Because you don't look like an anklet sort of guy, but I could be wrong. Where are my sister and father?"

"Where is my ring?"

Prince interjected with the obvious intention of keeping the situation under control. "We're here for a reason. Why don't you tell us what that reason is so we can cease all this unnecessary arguing?"

Vlad turned away from them and strolled toward the short wall. "How deep do you think that water is down there?" he asked conversationally.

Kat shot Prince a look of frustration, wanting to shove Vlad over the edge. "As deep as your compassion for others… so that would be pretty shallow."

Vlad wrapped his fingers around one of the suspension cables. "I don't know. Seems like you only need a few extra feet to drown."

A small spark of blue light escaped his fingertips and a scream ruptured the silence below. Her blood chilled.

"Nadia!"

Prince caged her with his arms, and the fierce wind whipped at them like punishment. His body was tense behind hers, his alpha power radiating off him like the sun warming her skin. It wasn't a calming energy, but one of rage, and she fed off that power. Kat reached beneath her shirt, ready to unsheathe her dagger and plunge it deep into Vlad's black heart.

"Won't do you any good, princess," he said mockingly. "I can move much faster than you." Vlad held a sharp blade in his hand, pressing it against a rope that was tethered to the cable. "The rope was up here before you arrived," he said, tapping the cable. "Seems to have slipped, but she's not going anywhere. The cable stops just below the wall, and it only takes one clean slice to send her on her way. She's suspended by her ankles, and her arms are bound. She won't be able to shift without breaking her wolf's legs. Unless you want to find out how long your sister can hold her breath, I suggest you hand me my ring."

"And I'm supposed to believe you'll just let her go? I wasn't born yesterday."

"I'll call off the bounty," Prince interrupted. "And that includes the men I have creating roadblocks on the interstate. We'll settle what's between us another time, but I give you my word you're free to go if you set down the knife."

"And what of my ring!" he bellowed, holding up a fist.

"Once the woman is pulled to safety, we'll make the trade."

Vlad gripped the cable again, and Kat couldn't be sure if he was sending a current of energy through it. "And what makes you think I can trust you won't come after me? Do you even *have* the ring with you?"

"I'll go with you," Prince said without hesitation.

Kat looked up at him in horror. Was a Packmaster really offering himself over as a sacrifice—risking his pack, his reputation, and his life... all for her? "You can't... You have a pack to run. I'll go."

"I'm more valuable to him. There's a score he's wanted to settle with me for centuries," he murmured before turning his attention to Vlad. "Take me as your hostage and I'll ensure you not only get your ring but leave the city safely. Free the girl; I can't trust you won't cut that rope once you have the ring in your possession."

Vlad drew in a heavy breath. "I never did like negotiators. It doesn't always go your way, Prince. Now hand it over."

Kat's heart raced so erratically that she had to hold her breath for a second to steady it. Nadia's life was hanging in the balance, and Kat refused to lose her sister over some cheap ring that meant nothing to her.

"Give it to him," she said, her voice cracking.

Prince moved in front of her, blocking out everything else and locking eyes with her. His hair was pulled back—like it always was—and she realized how much she preferred him in his usual clothes. The cargo pants and plain shirt made him look out of form, as if he were dressing up for Halloween. He'd never been anything less than himself, and that was the way she wanted him.

"Are you sure about this?" he asked in a quiet voice. "It's risky. Nothing comes that easy. He might do something drastic because he's afraid we'll chase after him."

She placed the flats of her hands on his chest. "I don't care. If he doesn't keep his word, then I'm ready to fight to the death. I'll do whatever it takes to save my sister's life. I can't quibble over a stupid ring. I know it gives us an advantage, but years ago I made a terrible decision that cost a man his life. I don't want to make the same mistake again. That's why I'm good at my job, Charming. I learn from my mistakes so I can make better choices. If he stabs me, then I'll shift to heal and let my wolf go after him. Save my sister, no matter what happens."

With a brisk nod, Prince turned around and reached in his leg pocket. He extended his arm—fist closed—and held Vlad's undivided attention with the promise of the centuries-old ring enclosed in the palm of his hand.

"Let me see it," Vlad said anxiously, a flicker of light sparking in his eyes.

Prince gracefully opened his hand and tilted it so the headlights shone on the gold ring with its ruby setting.

Vlad kept his knife on the rope. "Set it on the ledge and back away. Don't try anything stupid or I'll cut the rope."

Kat swallowed hard when Prince set the ring on the ledge and moved out of reach.

Vlad waited patiently before he snatched the ring and slid it onto his finger, then slowly made a fist. His shoulders sagged and he breathed out a heavy sigh. "So many years. You have no idea how powerful this is for a Mage. The craftsmanship is no longer to be found, and it has become invaluable with time."

"Put down the knife. We gave you the ring and kept our end of the bargain," Kat said, keeping her voice calm so as not to provoke him. "We're not coming after you; I just want to get my sister and go home."

I'll hunt your ass down another day, she thought to herself.

Vlad licked his lower lip, his gaze centered on Prince. "You won't last much longer."

Kat couldn't assess what was going on in Prince's head, but she just prayed he didn't say anything to set off this maniac.

Prince straightened his back. "I come from a powerful line of Shifters, and I'll outlive a worthless man such as you."

Kat sucked in a sharp breath when she saw the blade move. Tiny threads of rope sprang loose.

"Don't be so sure, my friend. War is in the air. Your puny little pack won't be able to stop the oncoming storm, and the best part is you animals will end up destroying yourselves, saving us the trouble."

"Those rumors have been circulating for eons, and that's all they are. Rumors invented by cowards."

Vlad smiled fiendishly. "Believe what you want." He dragged his eyes over to Kat, and her heart nearly stopped. "Your family has caused me nothing but grief for two hundred years. But I'm feeling generous tonight and would like to give you a choice."

"You said you'd let her go." Kat stepped forward, caught in a nightmare she couldn't control.

"And I will. That's a promise I will keep. If you look to your left on the other side of the divider, there is a rail. Further up is another rope with your father tied to the end. It's too far away for you to reach in time, but who knows? Maybe you're a fast runner. But you won't be able to save both. So what I'm curious to know is who do you love more, your sister or your father? Choose wisely, and we'll see each other again."

The sound of the blade cutting the rope was like the threads of her sanity shredding. She felt it all the way in her bones, and without time to process it all, she instinctively ran toward the wall. Kat jumped, her right foot propelling her off the ledge, and she leapt into the inky darkness.

Falling… falling.

Kat held her breath and shut her eyes as the sound of water exploded all around her. Her blood chilled when she penetrated the surface, and she imagined that this was what it felt like to die—so unbearably cold, so quiet. She opened her eyes, desperately trying to see in the murky waters.

Too dark. It's too dark.

A scream sounded underwater, and she swam toward it as hard as she could. Something touched her—coarse rope and smooth skin. Hair like spun silk enveloped her before she grabbed hold of Nadia's arm. Kat used her dagger to cut the rope, allowing Nadia to regain use of her hands and legs. When she had a tight grip of Nadia's waist, she swam upward.

At least, she hoped it was up. She moved toward a faint glittering of light, perhaps from the moon.

Nadia began to panic. Her body moved frantically and her lungs must have been screaming for oxygen. She'd given up whatever air she had left to call attention to herself when Kat had plunged into the water. Even in a chaotic situation, Nadia was always able to think clearly.

Kat's chest tightened as if an invisible hand were gripping it. The need to inhale became so intense that it became all-consuming.

Almost there, almost there, she repeated in her head, keeping her focused, keeping her alive.

They breached the surface and pulled in a hard gasp of air. Her lungs burned with sweet oxygen. Nadia was coughing as she struggled to catch her breath and stay afloat at the same time. Kat dipped below the water momentarily before surfacing again. She turned in a circle and looked at her surroundings, breathing heavily and trying to calm down so she wouldn't get muscle cramps.

The bridge stretched over them and they were close to the center. Kat swam in the direction where her father was supposedly tied up. Maybe Vlad hadn't gotten to him. As they kept swimming, Kat looked up, searching for someone swinging from the ledge, but in her heart, she knew he'd cut the rope.

As they neared the shore, Kat's tears were carried away by the river. She gasped at one point, wanting to just give up and sink to the bottom, but Nadia urged her on.

When they reached the shore, Nadia flipped onto her back, weak and out of breath. "Thank God, Katarina. *Thank God.*"

Every muscle in Kat's body screamed, but that dissipated when she raised her head and saw movement on the other side of the bridge. My God, she'd forgotten about Prince.

She swiftly got up and sprinted in that direction, stumbling over a rock. As she neared him, she began to process what was happening.

Prince hovered over her father—his hands locked together, delivering life-saving compressions. As she reached them, Prince stopped and blew another breath into his mouth.

Her father's gaunt features told a story of torture, but the rope tied around his ankles offended her most.

Kat fell to her knees, crippled with grief and guilt, blended together in a poisonous brew that threatened to pull her into a darkness from which she'd never come out of. Years of searching for her father... and she'd chosen to let him die.

"I drew the water out of his lungs," Prince said, starting another round of compressions. His wet shirt stuck to his body, and strands of hair had fallen from the band that held it.

Kat looked at her father's lifeless body. Shifters were hard to kill, but by no means were they immortal. Shifting allowed their body to speed up the healing process, so if they were injured, a few shifts would make them good as new. But if her father's heart had stopped...

"Papa!" Nadia shrieked, stumbling toward them. She put her arm around Kat, clinging to her and trembling with fright.

Prince blew another breath and then checked her father's pulse before he started compressions again.

Seconds turned into minutes. Nadia was shaking and whispering incoherently in Russian. Nothing could have prepared Kat for this moment, and she looked on in disbelief. She'd spent decades searching for her father, never giving up hope that one day they might be reunited. She wasn't ready to let him go. She reached down and took his hand, pressing it to her cheek.

"*Please,* Papa. Please… you can't die. Not like this. Not on the edge of a riverbank; it's not supposed to happen like this. I have to tell you I love you one last time. *Don't leave me.*" Tears burned her eyes as she kept repeating the last words.

When Prince began to tire, she pushed him away and took over. Kat had never learned CPR, but she'd just taken her first crash-course lesson by watching him. She went to blow a breath and whispered, "Please, Papa. Come back."

On her eleventh compression, he sputtered out a wet cough.

Prince pushed his eyelids up, his alpha voice becoming a fierce command. "*Shift.*"

Her father shifted into a red wolf, and once the healing magic began to take hold, Prince forced him to shift back. While he did this several times to help with the healing process, Kat fell back and covered her face with her arms. She'd never been so exhausted in her life, so overcome with emotions from opposite ends of the spectrum.

"He's going to be all right," Nadia whispered like a prayer.

Someone pulled Kat's arms away, and a dark shadow loomed over her. "Are you injured?" Prince asked.

"No."

"My apologies."

This was too much if he thought he was going to stand there and apologize. "What are you sorry for?"

"I made you a promise I wouldn't let Vlad get away, no matter what. I had to break that promise."

"You saved my father; you're off the hook. Where the hell did you learn CPR?"

He sat beside her and threaded a strand of wet hair away from her forehead. "I may be almost a thousand years old, but I know how to work a remote control, and I know how to perform CPR. Not every wolf can shift, and certainly not the children in my pack."

Kat reached out, cupping his cheek and stroking her fingers along his contoured features. "You're a remarkable man. I completely underestimated you."

"In what way?"

"So stupid," she said to herself, shaking her head. "I thought money meant you weren't as strong—that you have people do things *for* you. But you proved me wrong. It's not just that; it's everything. I shouldn't have judged you like I did, but most men with that much money and power don't really know how to live life or fight their own battles. I thought you'd go after Vlad—I really did. All that hate you have for him goes way back… I figured revenge would be more important to you than saving a man you haven't seen in centuries. Thank God you have long legs; you must've run really fast to reach him on time. I wasn't sure I'd be able to find Nadia underwater, and for a second there, I thought I was a goner."

He slid his hands behind her back and pulled her into a sitting position. "A woman like you is hard to kill. You're solid as a rock."

Kat burst out laughing. "Either you have a subtle sense of humor, or bad taste in music." She noticed the bewilderment in his eyes and stroked his arm. "Never mind." *Thank you*, she mouthed.

When Kat looked over her right shoulder, her father and Nadia were holding each other in a tight embrace. He'd put on his pants, and his raggedy button-up shirt was undone. He was the same man, but he appeared older because of his overgrown beard and gaunt appearance.

Damn Vlad for what he's done.

Her father turned toward her and she saw the spark of life in his eyes. It gave her a rush of satisfaction knowing Vlad hadn't won. He obviously didn't realize that he'd never be able to break Alexei Kozlov.

Her father reached out, curling his fingers inward and summoning her. "My Katarina…"

She crawled toward him and fell into his arms. Somehow her father's arms always felt like the strongest embrace in the world.

He loudly kissed her head, whispering to her in Russian. Guilt washed over her and splintered her heart. She couldn't bring herself to look up at him or speak a word.

He leaned back and lifted her chin with his fingers. "This is a happy night. Why the tears?"

"I… I had to choose." Her eyes flashed up to Nadia, who was standing behind him. Decades of longing for this reunion and now it was tainted with the insurmountable guilt of having left her father to die. Her chest tightened, and she struggled to breathe.

He patted her cheek. "And you chose wisely, little princess. Nadia is your other half, and I was always meant to go before either of you. A father should never outlive his children, and I'm proud of you. My two strong girls who will always exceed my expectations." He reached up and took Nadia's hand, pulling her closer to them. "I am a fortunate man."

Kat drew back when her father tried to stand. Prince watched but didn't help. She respected that. A man should be able to rise on his own two feet without someone's help.

He approached Prince and gripped his shoulders, giving them a hard shake before pulling him into a hug. "It's been a long time, my friend. I never thought I would see you again."

Prince made his hands into fists as he hugged him back, his eyes brimming with an emotion she couldn't read.

Her father let go and stepped back. "I hope you have built a good life for yourself."

"Why?" was all Prince managed to say. Kat knew his question held a deeper meaning—one that went back to her father giving him freedom in exchange for his own.

"Sometimes we are faced with the choice of saving ourselves or saving someone else. I did not feel my life held more value than yours at that time. I had no family. I had been hiding my fortune a long time ago, and my chances were better to financially recover if I could escape. Vlad wanted my money, but he wanted *you* dead."

Prince's hair had fallen from the band that held it back, and wet strands clung to his jaw. "I can never repay you."

Her father shook with laughter, bending over and holding his knees. Then he sharply cut off his laugh and looked up at Prince, his eyes resolute. "You fished me out of a river, my friend. My daughters are safe. Consider that debt paid."

Prince cursed under his breath. "I gave him the ring."

Kat stood up, water still in her shoes.

"It holds less value than he's built up in his head," her father replied. "Vlad obsessed over it because it represented someone outwitting him, but true, it does hold power. In this modern world, I don't think it will make him all-powerful. Anyhow, I have plans."

Prince wiped his face and stepped close. "And what plans are those?"

Her father sniffed and straightened his back, the edges of his shirt flapping in the wind. "I have missed my old friend, Prince. I think it's time that we go hunting together."

An enigmatic smile crossed Prince's expression and his eyes darkened. "You'll need your crossbow."

CHAPTER 15

"YOU'RE RUSTY, OLD FRIEND," PRINCE said, leaning against the rough bark of an elm tree.

Alex turned around and lowered his bow. "My wolf is not so rusty. We could always do this another way."

A distant voice wailed in pain, twigs snapping as the footsteps of their target faded into the distance.

"That would be too easy," Prince said, his voice menacing. "Where is the sport in that?"

Alex pulled another arrow from his quiver. "If at any time you begin to feel a scrap of pity for this man, then I will sit down and tell you about the numerous ways he tortured me and then made me shift to heal so he could torture me all over again."

Prince stepped over a fallen branch as they headed deeper into the woods. The sunlight illuminated the green leaves above, and they danced in the breeze like flecks of glitter. Most of the ground was covered with old leaves, wild ivy, and bushes. Only in the open areas did the high grass grow, but they were far from the open.

Alex seemed to have put on weight already. He was shorter than Prince, but had always had a robust physique. He'd trimmed his overgrown beard and added a little curl to the ends of his mustache. Alex had more grey in his hair than he should have at his age, but he'd lived a difficult life.

It hadn't taken long to capture Vlad after his escape. Reno had spoken with Greta and organized some associates of his to trace the vehicle. They'd found him at a gas station two miles outside Waco. From what Prince had been told, Vlad had used his ring. A shockwave of energy had destroyed the windows and batteries of two cars, but Vlad had been unable to escape after Reno plunged a stunner into his shoulder.

Instead of turning him in to the higher authority, Reno had discreetly given him over to Prince, who'd called Alex to help him decide what to do with him. They could collect a reward and watch him receive a death sentence.

Or… they could skip the formalities.

Prince and Alex were born in a different time, and when Alex had asked him how much property he owned, the decision became obvious. He remembered what Kat had said about her handcuffs neutralizing Breed powers—or at least those of a Mage—so he'd lifted them from her holster when she was in the shower. Prince needed them so Vlad couldn't use his Mage ability to heal with sunlight. She'd noticed they were missing right away but was uncertain whether or not she'd lost them during her jump off the bridge.

Alex had sent her and Nadia out to spend time together and bond. Everyone had enjoyed a nice dinner the night before after Prince had invited them to stay as his guests. Plenty of food, wine, and security, so the girls felt okay about leaving their father late that afternoon to complete some errands.

Prince and Alex had gone down to the basement where Vlad was lying paralyzed in the dirt, Reno's blade still lodged deep in his shoulder. Reno was the kind of man who didn't ask questions, and he seemed content knowing that Prince wasn't going to turn him over to the higher authority. All he wanted was his stunner back since they were hard for a non-Mage to come by.

Prince had placed one of the cuffs around Vlad's wrist and clicked it shut, then pulled the stunner from his chest, waiting to see if the cuffs really worked.

And they did. Vlad foolishly attempted to blast Prince with his power, but nothing happened.

So they led Vlad deep into the woods and—much to their surprise—he chose not to plead for his life but to curse their ancestors instead. Prince clenched his teeth together when Vlad made threats about what he was going to do to Kat's lifeless body—threats that no lover wanted to hear. And especially ones that no father was meant to hear. Alex struck him across the face with the tip of one of his arrows, leaving a bright streak of blood.

"Run."

An hour into the hunt, they shot him with a third arrow. They took their time, allowing him to flee and tire himself out. After each hit, they sat down and Alex smoked a hand-rolled cigarette, giving Vlad enough time to pull out the arrow and attempt to bandage the wound with scraps of his own clothing.

They continued down a short hill, following behind Vlad, who was moving slower than before.

The paper crackled when Alex took another puff. "Two shots do not make you a more expert marksman. You have made more attempts than I have. I will hit him when it counts."

"And I will strike him *where* it counts."

Alex laughed and patted out his cigarette. "Aha. Now I know why your hits were below the belt."

"And yours, Alex?"

The laugh died in his throat as they kept walking, the forest rustling below their feet. "I want my arrow to pierce his black heart."

"So then why did you shoot him in the back the last time?" Prince startled a squirrel when he ducked below a crooked branch.

Alex rubbed his short beard. "You can't remove the arrows very easily when you cannot reach them. I want Vladamir to suffer—to feel the twist of the arrow with every step, the same way he has twisted pain into my life. That coward threatened to kill my daughters, and no one who harms my children will live to tell about it."

In a swift motion, Alex took his position. He nocked the arrow and straightened his bow arm, drawing back the bowstring and quickly releasing it. The arrow sliced through the air with a sharp sound.

"This is a nice bow," he said admiringly. "I have always been partial to the crossbow, but these are good quality. Handmade?"

Prince swelled with pride as crafting recurve bows had been a hobby he'd enjoyed for many years. The younger Shifters were convinced that modern weaponry was better, but they didn't know the feel of holding a handcrafted bow that had been customized.

"Yes. I made these for my personal enjoyment, but I can make one for you if you wish."

Alex adjusted his armguard and stopped, his voice falling to a low volume. "I would very much like that." He rubbed his black-and-grey beard, staring ahead. "Vlad hasn't moved. It would be a shame if it was over so soon."

Prince turned his attention to the body slumped over in the ditch below. "There's something I wish to speak with you about." He shifted his stance, a cold sweat touching his forehead.

Alex turned to face him. "And what is that, old friend?"

Prince scratched the corner of his eye. Someone as old as him shouldn't have been so apprehensive about what he was about to say, and he knew his body language spoke volumes. "I've formed an attachment to your daughter."

A twig snapped beneath Alex's foot when he stepped forward. His chest moved as he silently hiccupped, and then he took a moment to light up a cigarette and pull in a few drags. "Nadia is a woman I could easily see by your side."

It took everything for Prince not to laugh. No disrespect to Nadia, but it came to his attention that Alex hadn't been perceptive about the way Prince and Kat had been looking at each other at the dinner table the night before.

"You should quit smoking," Prince said. "Kat's allergic."

Alex nodded while taking a last inhale. He patted out the end again and tucked it in his pocket. "Yes, strange thing. She's been that way since she was a little child. I remember once standing outside in a blizzard to have a cigarette because she made me. Didn't cry or complain while I smoked inside, but that little girl pushed me right out the front door and into the snow. Then she threw my pipe and matches onto the ground and slammed the door."

The thought danced in Prince's mind and he chuckled warmly. "That's what I love best about her."

Alex's eyes flashed up. "Kat? It's *Kat* you want? No... No, that cannot be. Katarina is my princess."

Prince lowered his eyes respectfully and bowed. "And I would like her to be mine."

He flinched when Alex slapped him over the back of the head.

"Nonsense. She is too strong for any man. Nadia is your kind."

His comment straightened Prince's spine like an arrow. "And what do you mean by that, Alex?"

"I love my daughters equally, but I have always had a special relationship with Kat. She is too strong for any one man. Nadia is driven by money and material things," he said with a wave of his arm. He swung his eyes up to a blue jay hopping on a nearby branch. "Kat makes money, but not to spend. She's very much like me in that she lives a humble life. She was always driven by love and loyalty."

"And that is why I've chosen her." Prince stepped forward, his voice resolute. "In all the centuries I've been alive, I've had nothing else to live for of substance. No mate, and while I may have once trivialized the matter, there is nothing trivial about Kat."

Alex had a way of dissecting a man with his stare. Prince stood his ground, never averting his eyes, and got a bone-deep fear that maybe his friend would forbid the pairing. Kat was still an adult who could choose her own destiny, but Prince respected old customs, which dictated that as long as her father was alive, Prince must win Alex's approval for the pairing.

And Prince was dead set about becoming mated. He had yet to find out if Kat was a woman easily won, but he had a feeling she'd make the chase hard, and that pleased him immensely.

Alex kept his steely eyes centered on Prince, tugging on his beard. "You are asking my permission for Kat?"

"I'm asking for your approval. I'll court her regardless of your answer, but I would like your blessing. As my friend, my brother, and—"

Alex burst out laughing. "And your *father*!" He patted Prince on the arm. "That would make us related in a most amusing way. For that reason, I approve. But you listen to me, old friend. If you hurt or deceive her, then *that* will be you," he said, pointing toward Vlad. "*Nyet*. I will not watch my daughter's heart be broken, and worse if it's by someone I trust. You think about that before you decide how serious you want to get with my Kat. My daughters are not the only royal blood remaining, and I can put you in contact with two other families who have daughters for you to consider."

The hell he would. Prince would love to have children with Kat, but none of this was about the purity of her blood; it was about the way he loved her and the way he wanted to love her.

With every ounce of respect he could summon in his voice, Prince answered. "I would be honored if you gave us your blessing, and you have my solemn vow as your friend and spirit brother that I will never cause harm to you or your family. I can assure you I will not only give Katarina the protection and security she deserves, but the love. I'm not a man who has warmed up to many women in my lifetime, and you know this more than anyone. But she's changed me... or awakened me. I have the greatest respect for the woman you've raised."

"And you would not want to change her? You would be a fool to try," he said, shaking his finger. "My Kat is a creature who cannot be reckoned with, and she would learn to hate the man who tried to shape her into a woman she is not."

"I would only suggest she consider a local job as a private investigator. She's an exceptional bounty hunter, but that would require too much travel and time away from her pack."

Alex began walking and they drew closer to the body. "Good luck with that if she agrees. I quit trying to change who she was when she was twelve and decided to learn how to shoot a gun." Alex playfully glanced at Prince over his shoulder. "She always had better aim than me."

"Then why does she carry a knife on her instead of a gun?"

"I made that holster for her a long time ago so it wouldn't fall off her wolf. I hid the ring inside, and that was partly the reason I made it. Kat is sentimental and I knew she would always cherish it because it was something I made special for her. But I never wanted her to be without protection. The stunner was a necessity because a Mage is hard to catch, and that left little room for a gun. She carried one, but then a man took it from her and shot her in the chest. It was hard for her to recover because the bullet was lodged inside, and that made a mess when she shifted. After that, she kept the gun in her car. I think in time she'll change her ways, especially if she moves to a state with a concealed handgun law," he said with a chuckle.

Prince lifted his chin. "She'll move here. I'm certain she'll accept my claim."

"And what will you do to win her heart?"

Prince considered it. "I'm taking her to a place called Cracker Barrel tonight for dinner before buying her something called peanut brittle."

Alex belted out a boisterous laugh. "There is hope for you after all, my friend. But it will take far more than food to win her devotion. You have your work cut out for you."

They stood next to Vlad's limp body, and Prince sighed, reflecting upon how many lives this man had destroyed in his lifetime. And for what? Power. Greed. Money. A stupid ring.

"Well, what do you want to do with him?" Prince asked.

Alex looked at the stretch of woods surrounding them. "Seems wrong to bury him on your land. There's evil in his blood, and it will taint the soil."

Leaves rustled, and Vlad exploded into action as he rose up and drove an arrow into Alex's leg. Prince kicked him in the chin, and the force caused him to fly back, blood spattering on his shirt from the open gash.

"No, no!" Alex yelled, holding out his left hand. "Leave him to *me*."

Alex pulled out an arrow and drew back his bow. He wore a black glove that covered his thumb and three fingers to protect them. The muscles in his arm tensed as he held position, lowering the tip of his arrow toward Vlad's heart.

Accepting his death, Vlad leaned back and laughed. "Go on and do it. No matter how hard you try to elevate yourselves, you'll never be more than sled dogs to us."

The arrow whistled as it sliced through the air and into Vlad's heart. He fell back, mouth agape.

Alex leaned forward and broke the arrow that had penetrated his leg. Blood flowed freely, saturating his pants as he pulled it free. He tore a strip of fabric from the bottom of his shirt and tied it over the wound. "I'll shift later—if I do it now, my wolf is liable to feast on his remains."

Prince fished the ruby ring from his pocket and it caught a flicker of sunlight. "What should we do with this?"

"Toss it into the river. Nadia would love an artifact such as that, and it would fetch a handsome price. But old magic like that should sink to the bottom where it belongs. Those trinkets weren't created to protect but to destroy. Someone will suffer because of that ring, so get rid of it."

"I'll have my men dispose of the body. Do you want me to finish him off?"

Alex pulled out his hunting knife and inspected each side. A Mage didn't die easily, and there was no guarantee Vlad wouldn't draw healing energy from the sunlight and rejuvenate, so the custom was to remove the head from the body.

Alex squatted next to Vlad's lifeless body and looked up at Prince. "This is personal. He took my freedom more than once and tried to take my sanity. Then he took my child. Now I will take his head."

Prince dropped the ring back in his pocket and turned away. "And if Kat calls, where do you want me to tell her you are?"

A low chuckle rose from behind. "If my Kat calls, you tell her I'm taking the head of my enemy. If Nadia asks, tell her... tell her I'm fishing."

CHAPTER 16

———————————

"You're an exceptional snuggler, Charming," Kat said. "Anyone ever tell you that?"

She melted when Prince shifted his body behind her to press himself even closer. She loved the way they fit together, the way his hands memorized every curve, the way he smelled, the feel of his strong heart beating against her back and picking up tempo whenever she did something as simple as stroking his hand.

His breath heated her ear, his words playful. "This is the most unusual date I've been on."

She stuck her right toe into her left sock and pulled it off. "Casual is always the way to go. Pizza, fresh brownies, and *Die Hard* movies wrapped up with a *Three's Company* marathon? You've been missing out."

"I have to admit, I'm intrigued by Chrissy Snow."

Kat peered over her shoulder. "Maybe it's because of her big tits."

She shivered when he covered her mouth and scolded her with his mismatched eyes. "I think it's how she always gets the wrong idea. It reminds me of someone."

She licked the palm of his hand until he pulled it away. "Oh, really? Who? Because I don't remember ever—"

"On the rooftop with your sister. I still believe you would have crashed onto our table, regardless if Vlad was there or not."

She turned on her back, her knees bent. Kat wasn't sure where her father would end up moving and whether or not she would follow, but she knew she had to make a career choice soon, and that fork in the road was a lot more frightening close up. "So… where are we going with this? I've been staying with Nadia for a week and dividing my time between you and my father."

Prince traced his finger over one of her eyebrows. "Has he decided if he wants to settle here and start a pack or move elsewhere?"

"He's been out of the loop for a while. You can imagine how hard it'll be for him to get a good second-in-command to help build a pack. That takes time, and he sure doesn't want someone's leftovers. He won't go rogue either, but it's a lot to figure out for a man who's starting over again. He's been living in basements for the past twenty years, so maybe he deserves a short vacation before immersing himself in pack politics."

"I spoke to your father about us."

Kat's throat instantly dried up and her heart skipped a beat. She suddenly had visions of her father hunting Prince in the woods.

He stroked her cheek and then rested his hand beside her, twirling a lock of her hair between his fingers. "He balked about it for a few seconds, but Alex is a fair man. He won't deny you something if it's what you desire."

"So what does this mean? You're a dapper guy, but you're not making any big moves, and I have to get back to my job."

"I'm courting you, Kat. That means you're the only woman in my sights, and I have intentions for this to end with a mating ceremony. We've been casual for the past week because of how fast things were moving, and I wanted to slow down and let you focus on your family. But now that we've watched a sitcom together, this needs to move to the next level."

Hearing those words from his lips was like a clap of thunder. What they had was more than attraction, unbelievable sex, or wishful thinking; his claim was a declaration of intent. Wolves mated for life, and Prince was openly inviting her into his pack to live their lives together.

Earlier that week, he'd formally introduced her to his wolf—a handsome black-and-grey animal with mismatched eyes. The moment he shifted, one of his packmates reactively pulled Kat away, and Prince's wolf lunged at him. Prince had protected her in both human and wolf form, and she knew he was a man she could trust completely. But Kat wasn't raised to be easy prey for any man, and she wanted the courtship to be long so she could be certain she wasn't just caught up in the moment.

"Do you love me?" she asked. Wondered. Hoped. Feared. Never had a single word roused so many emotions.

His lips brushed against hers and she straightened her legs, a flame of desire heating her body. "If I've not said the words aloud in the right way, then let it be known, Katarina Kozlov, that you have ensnared my heart. I've never given those words to a woman. My love is steadfast, and I vow to never smother the proud alpha that you are. You'll help me lead my pack, and I'll pluck the moon from the heavens if it pleases you."

Kat's heart warmed, and as much as she wanted to tease him for waxing poetic, she couldn't. That was who Prince was, and that was exactly what she admired about him. Even the fact that he was snuggled behind her in a tie gave her goose bumps because it just meant more of him to undress.

"And do you, Katarina, love me?"

"Yep."

He tapped her nose. "Just *yep?*"

She curled her hands behind his neck, and he rolled halfway onto her in response. "I like you, Charming. I really do. But I'm not going to lie. The love you give to me feels so… undeserved. You love me so perfectly, but I don't know how to love you the way you deserve to be loved. You should be seduced by an oiled-up woman wearing a bustier and a thong, not lying on a sofa watching sexual innuendos from the seventies."

His eyes glittered when she laughed softly. "You've already found the way to my heart, Kat. Just keep doing what you're doing and we'll meet somewhere in the middle." He eased up on his elbows. "Will your sister have trouble accepting my intentions with you? I don't want to be the cause of a rift."

With that lovely thought, Kat scooted to a sitting position.

Prince had converted one of the rooms in his mansion just for her. He must have tired of her complaining about his pristine sofas, so he'd purchased a plush one from a discount store and had it thoroughly steam cleaned. Kat didn't feel like she had to spot-check her clothes before sitting, and she wanted to feel completely at home when she was around him. That was hard to do when sitting on a snow-white sofa. He had taken the time to decorate the room with furnishings he thought she'd enjoy, such as a popcorn machine in the corner and posters of television shows she'd mentioned were her favorites. Kat didn't even know TV shows made posters, but when he'd revealed the room to her, she'd laughed so hard that she nearly peed her pants.

Not to mock him, but because she was so floored by how much thought he put into everything he did for her. He'd even bought her a pair of running shoes with short laces. Just thinking about those thoughtful gestures, she realized she could love a man like him forever.

Kat curved her hand around his arm and held on. "Nadia's going to be fine. You were right. We had a long talk, and she's not interested in you."

His brows popped up and it made her chuckle.

"I don't mean that in a bad way, only that she was more swept up with the idea of you than whether or not there was a connection. I think her friend Naya is setting her up on another date this weekend, so you're in the clear." Kat turned her attention to the television and laughed at a scene before looking back. "Why didn't my father try to contact you after he escaped from Russia? I tried to ask him about it, but he doesn't want to talk about that part of his life."

Prince began rolling up the sleeves of his dark blue shirt. "We spoke privately about this after Vlad's capture. I don't think I'll ever understand his decision; I wasn't raised to make selfless choices, and he was only a good friend, not family. Not by blood nor by pack."

"Sometimes people put their lives at risk for strangers, Charming. It's just the right thing to do, and for him, I'm sure he saw no other choice."

Prince nodded, reaching around and removing the band from his ponytail. Kat's toes curled when he shook loose his dark hair and let it fall over his shoulders.

"When I asked why he didn't search for me after his escape, he admitted he'd been living in hiding for decades, and he was ashamed. While he'd found his freedom, he knew Vlad would search for him because of that ring. The world was much bigger then, Kat. We couldn't look up someone on the Internet or in a phone directory. When he moved to America, Cognito was a city Breed naturally gravitated to. He heard my name in certain circles but decided there was a reason our lives had diverged in the same way that they had once intersected. He said if fate meant for us to rekindle our friendship, then it would make plans."

"Huh," Kat remarked. "It makes you wonder about all the coincidences in life. I met you because I followed my father's old nemesis to town, but how did you meet Nadia?"

When his face turned scarlet, she scooted toward him excitedly. This looked too juicy to ignore.

He cleared his throat and attempted to focus on the TV. "There was a woman I foolishly made an offer to because she would have been an ideal match."

"You mean the whole pureblood thing, right?" Kat straightened his tie, itching to run her fingers through his wonderful hair.

He lifted his chin as if he didn't deserve her affection. "She denied me for another man. When I went to extend my congratulations while tending to other business matters, Nadia was there. We were introduced, and I couldn't help but ask about her surname. It was then that she mentioned a name I hadn't heard in over two hundred years. So I offered her a ride home."

"I like the sound of that. Let's steal that story and make it ours."

"And why would I do that?" he asked, pulling her onto his lap so that she was straddling him.

Kat offered him a sultry smile and shrugged. "People might ask how we met, and you'll get embarrassed telling them that I crashed your date with my twin, shared cold pizza with you on the sofa, dragged you to a rundown bar where I zipped up your pants, and got you into a bar fight with a Mage."

His ardent kisses trailed along her neck and she rocked her hips, dark hunger gnawing her from within. "On the contrary, that's the best story I can think of. Except you left out the part where you got naked on top of another man."

"You smell nice," she whispered, licking her lips. She slid her hand around to the nape of his neck and gave his hair a gentle tug.

"And what do I smell like?"

"Yummy."

When he broke the kiss, she pouted and gave him a disapproving look.

It was hard to stay mad for long when she looked into his brown and blue eyes, perfectly framed by his dark brows and lashes.

"I have some news. Do you remember Reno?"

She nodded and tried to catch her breath, wondering how anyone could be in the midst of a passionate moment and just pull away to start discussing other men.

Prince placed his hands on her thighs and gave them a light squeeze. "It looks like Reno's going to need some help. The higher authority reviewed the files you sent from Vlad's computer, and they've officially declared several men outlaws they were previously unable to identify. Two left the state, but a couple are still living in the area. They also passed along information regarding local trading rings and offered Reno a substantial amount of money to investigate and break them up. But he can't do it alone, and I suggested you might be interested. I think it will be good for you to establish strong connections in our territory and complete a big case to build your reputation."

"Are you serious?" she exclaimed, gripping the collar of his shirt and tugging. "You got me a job working with a PI?"

"I secured you a job *as* a private investigator, if you want it. You'll partner with Reno as a temporary situation. He thinks if you help bring in a few of these outlaws that it'll be substantial enough to get you some cases of your own. Word of mouth is the best advertising, or so I've heard."

Kat kissed his chin, the hard bristles of his short whiskers rough against her lips. "It's a dangerous job. Sometimes I have to get up in the middle of the night and leave, and occasionally I might go out of town, but not often. Mostly the jobs are local; I've known a few

PIs, and they told me all about their cases. It's not all dangerous. Sometimes I'll be helping abused kids or going undercover to find out if an employee is stealing from his boss."

Prince kissed her lavishly, his arm encircling her waist. "Make the world a better place, Kat."

"You'd still want to pursue me despite the dangers?"

His brow arched. "If we're being honest, then yes, I have a problem with knowing you risk your life every day for strangers. And if any man threatens you in my presence, I can't promise I won't blow your cover by snapping his neck."

She kissed him hard, tasting his conviction in every stroke of his tongue. It was decadent, and the way he handled her was the way every woman dreamed of. She could feel the desire and reverence in the way his hands discovered the gentle curve of her hips, her round breasts, and the soft skin beneath her shirt. Kat had spent her life capturing men, and it looked like one had finally captured her.

She moved her hand down to his pants and decided she despised belts. "Next time I want you in sweatpants."

A knock sounded at the door.

"Come in," Prince murmured between kisses.

Since when did Prince become affectionate in public? Suddenly Kat went shy and hopped off the couch, putting distance between them.

Russell poked his head in, his eyes downcast in the dark room. "They've baked a roast downstairs if you'd like me to bring up a plate."

Kat put her hands on her hips, watching Prince from the corner of her eye. "No, tell everyone we'll be coming down to dine with the pack."

Prince's eyes widened. He didn't socialize with his pack and took most of his dinners in his room while permitting the pack to eat together and bond. One thing Kat knew about the ancients was that they believed becoming too personal with other wolves would make them lose their fear of the Packmaster, and fear was power. But nothing was more powerful than family. It was time for him to change, and Kat was just the person to give him a nudge.

Russell cleared his throat, dismissing Kat's order and looking at Prince for guidance.

"You heard the lady," Prince said.

She smiled and gave Russell a smug look of satisfaction before terrifying him with her sad attempt at a Scottish accent. "So shut yer geggie and dust off his chair, because we'll be dining with the fam tonight." Kat snapped her fingers, her voice returning to normal. "By the way, I got something for you."

Kat jogged behind the sofa and reached for a thick box wrapped in red paper. It was about the size of a dictionary. She strolled across the room and handed it to Russell, who had inched farther inside. "It's just a thank-you gift for all your help with finding Vlad."

He shook the box and heard several hard objects rattle at once. His expression tightened. "Is this what I think it is?" he said with annoyance, tilting the box and listening to it rattle once more. "I'll tolerate your Scottish jokes and poor attempt at slang, but this is where I draw the line."

"Open it."

He tore the paper away, letting it fall to the floor. Russell's eyebrows knitted together as he read the writing on the yellow box. "*Whitman's* chocolates?"

Kat rocked on her heels, a broad smile on her face. "I never did like Russell Stover. There are two layers in this one, so if you don't like the coconut or toffee ones, feel free to slide them onto my dinner plate later tonight."

He laughed heartily and scratched the back of his neck. "Aye, I'm sorry I ever called you a name. You're a bonnie lass with a big knife, so I'll say my thanks and go dust off that chair." Russell closed the door and left them alone.

Kat sauntered toward the sofa and took a seat to Prince's left. "My father was the same way with his pack; he never ate with them. I've never been in a pack of my own, but I know it strengthens the bonds when the Packmaster is there to break bread with his packmates. I think you should consider it. If you're not comfortable with socializing, then I'm not going to make you change your ways. But if this works out between us and someday we end up mated, then I'll probably be dining with the pack. I don't want to segregate myself upstairs so they can live in fear of me. I'm changing my whole life for you, and all I'm asking is for you to try one thing."

Prince was rather tall in comparison to Kat, so she found herself trying to sit up straighter. He wrapped his arm around her and held her close.

"You've made concessions for me, and I will do the same. But I'll only do what makes me comfortable. If eating with the pack doesn't go well, then I'll resume my current routine."

"I think you should give them a chance," she said. "I'm sure they're great people, but that whole mentality of a pack living in fear isn't the best way to run a house. Well, maybe it's not about the best or worst way… only that it can work either way. So why not do the one that's more fun? Don't you know any Packmasters who dine with their packmates?"

"Yes," he replied in a husky voice.

"And do you think their packmates respect them less?"

He pursed his lips, his eyes still on the television. She sensed he didn't want to be proven wrong.

Kat grasped his chin and turned his head to face her. "I know you've got a mad crush on Chrissy Snow, but I'm over here."

Prince reached for the remote and switched off the TV, immersing them in darkness.

Her body dragged down the cushions, and he settled his weight on top of her. Nothing felt better—nothing in the whole world. She lifted her hips, feeling the hard length of him as his heart pounded against her chest in anticipation.

"We're going to be late for dinner," she whispered against his ear.

Prince unfastened her jeans, his lips against the soft spot on her neck, his body shaking with desire. "Yep."

41220540R00112

Made in the USA
San Bernardino, CA
01 July 2019